Ralph Bartholdt's writing and photography have appeared nationally and in regional publications throughout the Pacific Northwest. His work has been recognized by the Idaho Press Club, National Newspaper Association, the Associated Press and the Society of Professional Journalists. He lives in Idaho's Panhandle.

Also by
RALPH BARTHOLDT

Sometime, Idaho
Somewhere, Idaho
someplace, Idaho

"Paintin' ol' Jesus, she's a self feeder!"

— Johnny Bedore

Tank Creek

Short essays from the Panhandle

Grassy Mountain Press
St. Maries, Idaho

For permission requests write to Grassy Mountain Press, grassymountainpress@gmail.com

ISBN: 979-8-218-07658-0 (Paperback)

Library of Congress Control Number: 2022917578

Portions of this book are works of nonfiction. Some of these essays have appeared in another form in *Northwest Sportsmen Magazine, Idaho Magazine, The Lewiston Tribune and Coeur d'Alene Press.*

Photos by Ralph Bartholdt unless otherwise noted.

Johnny Bedore quote from "Up the Swiftwater" by Sandra A. Crowell and David O. Aslesen

Book design by Benjamin Riley.

Printed by kdp.amazon.com

First printing edition 2022.

Grassy Mountain Press

Uncle Jim

Contents

Heat

Hunting

Snow

Break Up

Heat

TANK CREEK

Maps on the Table

Clutter to her is the most vile of civil conditions.

Est le pire, in the language of some of our forebears. It's a scourge.

On kitchen counters clutter of any kind must be especially avoided because counters are made for the glistening and lemon fresh goodness of white quartz and sunshine.

Clutter is a cloud that reflects disharmony, a lousy upbringing. It reveals a lack of planning, culture and garage space.

It is as far from *feng shui* as a serrated knife stuck in a stick of butter.

Those of us who would add a biscuit to that combination, and jam, or sausage gravy take for granted her truck shop roots that accept dirty boots and gloves with a shrug if they stay in the mud room, and cheap beer if it stays in the crisper.

But clutter? Nuh-uh.

We must pause and appreciate the degree of her suspirations.

Given her aversion to stacks of newspapers in the living room, shotshells, pocket knives, billfolds, sunglasses, junk mail and dog collars that collect on kitchen counters it was prodigious in its own subtle way that the map, a big forest map like a carnival accordian, was allowed to lay open on the counter for months.

A felt marker rested nearby and a laptop displaying a satellite image was part of the combination. They nudged the wine rack containing a dusty bottle of unopened Merlot from Christmas, and a half empty bottle of cowboy whiskey from a couple of paydays ago.

The map showed the roads we needed to reach the remote places we planned to go.

The route was marked with a yellow highlighter, and from 15,000 feet the laptop screen showed the backwood trail leading to water where we surmised not a lot of people cast for trout.

We weren't certain, but a couple of river guides concurred. Foot traffic diminished proportionally with distance from the gravel road, they said.

Our chances of hooking at least a few big fish that hadn't seen an imitation caddis since gasoline prices lived south of two bucks were nominal.

It was spring when I visited the fly shop and sat around a table with fingers squeezed into the rings of a coffee cup inhaling the dander from feathers and elk hair that wafted from a fly-tying table.

Harmless snowflakes fell outside like peacock herl and

the guides who joined me at the table expounded on that particular river. They shared stories of overnight stays, the crackle of kindling and fish the size of violin cases before the pause of reflection swirled down a memory hole.

Their minds returned to considering a livelihood that shuttled anglers by the seatload to what they referred to as "road water," both agreeing their work required keeping a little bit of northern Idaho to themselves.

One of them, who was lean as a twig and sported a dark brown beard when he began the guiding business twenty years ago, now massaged a burly stomach under a bonefish shirt and whiskers gray as a seasoned pointer.

He waited until the shop had emptied before leaning on the cash register to reminisce. He once walked miles of that river from first light to dusk, lifting fat pigs from under cut banks and not seeing another angler.

"That was a good day," he said.

He won't take sports to those reaches simply because it's too far out, and most of them prefer to fish from the cab of a pickup truck, or a boat seat and its braces.

Clients appreciate the rugged luxury of air conditioning, ice-packed coolers and magnetic fly rod holders, he said.

"It's another dimension where you're going."

When a man and woman walked through the swinging front doors of the shop wearing sunglasses, ski jackets and fur-topped boots to address the late spring snowfall, he barked at them from behind the cash register.

"Let me know if you need anything!"

I slipped through the door into the outside glare, and it wasn't much later that spring had turned to summer with solstice falling off the refrigerator calendar. She and I had settled on a departure date and a couple of landing zones we would use to reach the river that was solidly tongue and grooved into Idaho wilderness.

In the meantime, our counter like Sunday potluck had attracted an additional host of accouterments.

Tippet and leader, shorter than the usual nine footers, probably from a clearance rack. A pile of ugly imitation bugs hand-tied in Montana that looked like caddis casings; mono and fluorocarbon in assorted weights and colors; high tenacity polymers with excellent knot strength. Clippers joined a spool of sink tip line and empty fly boxes with the price tags still on them. It also collected a few pairs of polarized sunglasses likely pulled from under a car seat or from the inside of a jockey box behind the manual that showed where to put the oil and how to find the tire jack.

A boat net with a rubber basket leaned against the counter like a broom. Its handle was walnut, curly maple and myrtle wrapped in paracord.

Thermoses appeared. One was blue endorsing the local football team and another, slender, was likely better suited for a hike.

A bag of trail mix. Protein bars. Insoles for her wading shoes.

"Just keeping it real," she said.

A cigarette lighter charging cord for a GPS watch was

wrapped around a ceramic coffee mug with a painting of a yellow humpy dry fly.

A friend who heard about our plan left a dozen attractor patterns big enough to hang a dropper.

You think we should tie some tungsten worms? she asked, meaning San Juans.

That would require setting up the vice and buying beads, so no, she decided, we'll use what we have.

This plan also kept the counter free for even more clutter.

And then, as if a fairytale clock struck midnight we looked at ourselves and the piles of stuff on the counter and smiled.

The night we prepared to go, after months of planning, we drank coffee from nondescript mugs, rinsed them and turned them upside down on a dish towel next to the sink.

We popped open cans of seltzer, sipped, then threw the empties into the recycling.

We counted the gear on the counter, packed it into containers, bags and backpacks, stowing it with a reasonable assumption we would find what we wanted, when we wanted it.

The clock's big arms ticked as we lay in bed with the windows open clinging to the last of the day's cornucopia, a kaleidoscope of events, maps and check-marked lists.

With our eyes ready to flutter into dark distance like pine moths, and the western sky a napkin smear of light, she turned.

She rolled sideways and I felt a bump and nudge.

Somewhere on the highway a car's engine revved.

"What will we do with the dog?" she asked.

Two Handed Fisherman And The River

As a kid living in a small room in a log house on a lake in the North Woods, a box of outdoor magazines that a preacher gave me from his garage was a treasure trove.

Mayflies, caddis and stones fluttered against the window screen at night and little brown bats bumped and crawled on the mesh chasing them. Magazine stories by Russell Annabel and Corey Ford kept me in suspense more than the bats.

Coleman lanterns hissed in the living room and the sallow light of the sooty oil lamps with glass chimneys cast long shadows across walls. Outside the last of the walleye fishermen bobbed on black water before reeling their lines, twisting the throttle on their outboards and heading home.

It was in that room of the log house with a never-ending hush of waves against the rocky shore that I discovered, between the magazine pages, a river on the other side of the divide called The Rockies, weeks away on foot, maybe months. The river flowed west from the Bitterroots of Lewis and Clark fame to the Pacific Ocean and it was filled with a special fish that part of the year traveled this river like a highway from the Pacific coast to its spawning grounds in the mountains.

The river was named Clearwater and the magazine ran a double page watercolor of a man, solo and chest deep in a quiet pool surrounded by floating leaves under a sky gray as laundry.

He was fishing for sea-run steelhead trout.

This river was relatively undiscovered, said the author. It was known to locals and the determined few, including Russell Chatham, the Western painter, writer and world class fly angler.

Later, when I rolled into northern Idaho as a teenager, I didn't immediately try to recapture the image of the fly angler standing waist deep casting for steelhead.

I had more or less forgotten it, and the country was too big, with too many distractions. Elk bugles and drop-tined mule deer, blue ribbon trout water, and high mountain fire lookouts shared with billy goats the cliffs that dropped to other iconic rivers with names such as Snake and Salmon.

Twenty years after I dug in the preacher's silverfish-infested box of garage magazines, I finally and purposefully rumbled south from Idaho's panhandle through a string of small towns that hugged forests and rolling prairie. I hung a left through the community of Potlatch, which appeared twined to an ebbing timber industry and trying to recover from a long belch of down and out. I turned through Deary, another relic looking for a way out of stump heaven, and shot the Kendrick grade like a flume. Near the shrunken downtown of Juliaetta I wound a steep road that took me over a hump of wheat to the river I had read about. The river that for centuries has been a stream of contentment no matter how hard the times.

I drove through Lenore on the river road, crossed the community's old bridge and skirted remnants of agriculture and rail. They invoked a yearbook memory of gangly basketball boys with freckles on their backs and cheers following the Pledge of Allegiance in a small, sweaty, high school gymnasium.

At the Peck turnoff I swung right onto a dirt road.

Near a stand of tall firs, I veered right again, hard this time, to a mud and gravel yard where I parked on a scab of dewy grass between two, trailered drift boats.

A dog barked as I slid from the pickup's seat and stood stretching in a wash of autumn air that was golden with the perfume of fir and fallen leaves.

I walked up the steps into a small, barnlike building appropriately called The Red Shed.

It was cool inside. A heater hummed. Lights were low. The walls rung with fly gear.

No one was there.

I walked outside and squinted into the morning sun.

Wagging its tail in a show of hesitancy and ownership, the dog, a spotted and fluffy farmyard mix, barked a steady stuccato that said "Hello, hold tight, because Poppy is on his way."

Then I saw a man with a beard like a gnome in sweatpants and baseball cap picking his way around potholes as he walked the driveway from a nearby doublewide.

"Hi," I said.

"How are you?" Poppy replied.

Poppy, the man, the legend, known to his family and the state licensing bureau as Mike Cummins, is not large. Years have given him the girth of a sea-run salmon ready to pound water if hooked. He is the compact kind of big with a beard that covers a quarter of him. Like the fish that he chases, and teaches others to catch – the ones that run this river to the sea and back – he has traveled some. A contractor for much of his life, and a trucker until he called it quits to follow the divining rod of his intuition, Poppy converted a small tack shed into a business that specializes in something special.

He started a fly shop dedicated to two-handed fly rods before the sport of North American spey casting had really taken off.

He did it because he loved the rods, the river and steelhead, and because of his arthritis.

"I was trying to spread the pain around," he says.

Fishing for steelhead with heavy fly rods had become

untenable, but Poppy knew there were men much older than he, in far off places, who waded rivers and caught hard-fighting sea-run fish using very long rods. They smiled at the endeavor without grimacing for the ache in their shoulders and back.

He researched and found a method of lake fishing in the British Isles that used "Loch" rods. These were large, two-handed varieties that could zing gear, but they were made for standing water.

More research brought him to spey: Two handed rods as long as sixteen feet that can cast far and easily mend a lot of line for a good presentation on swiftly moving water.

Because he couldn't afford to purchase a custom-made spey rod, he built his own out of spare Fenwick parts and some graphite tubing.

He called it the "junkyard spey," and it still hangs in his Red Shed fly shop on the Peck cutoff road to remind him of the days when he didn't have the cash to buy what he now sells.

"Our focus here is pretty narrow," Poppy says. "It's all two-handed rods."

And because the pocketbooks of most of his neighbors aren't bulging with lucre, he sells spey packages at moderate prices. The rods come with lifetime warranties.

"I don't sell any that aren't guaranteed for life," Poppy says. "I know most people are working people and they can't drop a thousand dollars for a two-handed rod."

This part of the world, despite its blue-ribbon cutthroat trout fisheries – Kelly Creek lies to the east – is often spin-cast country. That means swivels and snap hooks, lead sinkers thrown from boats with twin engines, chrome and aluminum hulls that leave wakes sloshing the shoreline.

It's a chunk of trot line heaven, but the game wardens troll the river too.

Anglers standing in the water hip-deep throwing line toward the opposite bank are becoming more frequent.

Despite his countenance, ample beard and long rod, Poppy doesn't stand out much in this community. He has become a staple of this river landscape and is less an anomaly than his clients that hail from the coast to Colorado and east to the Battenkill. They arrive in cars with out-of-state plates because they too, probably and maybe long ago, read the magazine article I read, or the many online pieces that have since appeared lauding the veracity of this river tucked into Idaho's crevasses.

The series of migrations that bring anadromous fish to this inland region, often coinciding with autumn colors, don't attract oodles of anglers and the river even now is mostly underutilized.

The locals like it that way.

Fishers who throw spey stop at the Red Shed where Poppy gives them a hat with a logo of a small red barn to advertise his business, and he gives them advice.

He doesn't push or pull.

His teaching is steadfast and his long rods are appealing for their friction-defying machinery.

Upriver from Poppy's, the big dam at Ahsahka, a towering concrete wall with midnight lights and the collaboration of multiple government agencies, impounds more than three million acre-feet of the North Fork of the Clearwater River. Stretching fifty miles and covering seventeen thousand acres, the impoundment is home to warm water species such as bass, and also colder water, landlocked salmonids. The reservoir is a boon to boaters and summer recreationists. Historically, a large strain of steelhead traveled this part of the river too, but the dam, built without ladders, has prevented upstream travel to migrating fish for a half century.

Chatham likened the dam's finality to a fiery auto wreck with no survivors. The writer Jim Harrison targeted this impoundment in a novel memorable if only for Harrison's prognostic vision of the Rocky Mountain West.

After the dam was built and the reservoir formed in the 1970s, a band of elk from the region's renowned wapiti herd walked on winter ice, broke through and drowned. The tragedy is still recalled by residents who grumble about the subterfuge that fueled the dam project and how, in the end, the Ahsahka dam was at best a boondoggle.

And what Chatham and Harrison were getting at.

Poppy doesn't spend much time on politics.

He elects to cast for the often massive and bullish sea-run trout to capture their majesty, if for a moment, and touch their secrets.

At every opportunity this feat is consummated with a long rod in memory of the junkyard spey.

TANK CREEK

Old School

I know a woman who heats cold pizza in a stove and yesterday's coffee in a saucepan.

Nuke it, I tell her. It only takes a minute.

No, she says. This way is better.

Old school.

Today on Main Street I looked into a bucket.

"What is it?" the man asked.

The bucket was in the back of his pickup truck and inside it was a fish.

"Not a carp," I said.

"Nope," said the man.

He was sawed off and his knuckles were white from years spent turning wrenches while laying on his back under logging equipment. Or, with half his body dipped into the loins of a crawler tractor, or the engine compartment of a tractor trailer where the slip of a ratchet rapped knuckles on angle iron or cold, hardened steel. The bloodletting caused pain that later turned white.

"It has gold skin and a red eye," he said.

"Not a native fish," I said.

He wore rigging jeans and suspenders and his hickory shirt was half zipped revealing a chest of gray hair and blubber.

"Could be a tench," I offered.

"Not a tench," he said.

He used to catch tench in a pond on the Shoshone and Benewah County line as a boy. Caught lots of them, but this was no tench, he assured.

His pickup was parked in front of the local bait and tackle and the owner came out for a look.

"Geezus Charlie," the owner said. "How come you're keeping these tench?"

Charlie had caught tench, or doctor fish, way back in the '50s and didn't think the fish in the bucket in the back of his pickup resemble what he remembered about the Eurasian imports.

"I used to catch them as a kid," he said.

"Well," said the bait and tackle shop owner. "This one may have been around when you were a kid."

The dead fish, a few pounds and a foot or two long, red-eyed and golden- skinned, lay curled to accommodate the bucket.

"They are all about the same size," said the bait and tackle shop owner. "Even the ones as old as you."

He winked to make the point, then grinned.

"Waddya catch it with?"

"Worm."

That's old school.

Not far upriver from Calder, I cast a dry fly in a run that made a bottleneck below a bank and hooked a few small fish the color of tourmaline.

I wasn't satisfied, and because I had gotten a late start, the western sky already slicked orange.

I tied on a streamer with a bull head that, tossed right, shouted, "Olé!"

Nudging my way up the water, I found it warm as the Parisian canals where tench probably vie for Euros flipped by tourists for luck.

One, two, three casts and I hooked a cutthroat trout bigger than the earlier ones. Still wanting more, I nudged deeper into the current like a poacher tossing a spoon under the overhanging limb of a river birch.

Way out there with my nine-foot fly rod, a plastic fly box hanging with a lanyard from my neck, I made a beautiful looping mend at which no one but me could marvel.

I wore jeans and a tank top. Occasional drivers of cars bumping past honked their horns.

"That's no fly caster," they said. "He's not wearing rubber pants."

"He's whipping whatever is on that line."

"There's a beer can in his back pocket."

Not every fly fisher keeps an H. L. Leonard credit card, or has darkened the door of the Oman Fin Club with a Cuban Montecristo gripped in his teeth.

Some of us just want to drive a dirt road in a beat up Sunbird to hook fish.

Wet or dry, it doesn't matter.

The cafe by the bridge has brews to go, and Swisher Sweets with plastic tips.

That's old school.

T100

I once followed a T100 across the state of Montana.

The pickup was white with straw stuck to the manure that smeared a fender.

When it gained speed east out of Deer Lodge like a colt chasing its fence line, swirls of hay and grain husks lifted from its bed.

A woman was behind the wheel. She wore a fleece collared denim jacket.

For hours, we followed each other, back and forth, while other vehicles, coupes, cruisers and SUVs, passed with neurotic indifference using one freeway exit to gain another. They boasted gallery license plates, pieces of art tightly screwed to frames that advertised car dealerships often from another state.

My plates said Idaho in a smear of red, white and blue.

Hers were the light blue rainbow plates from decades earlier with "Big Sky" written in cursive across a corner covered as it were with horse hockey.

We rolled over the Great Divide like the sweeping lull of cloud shadows, sinking in and out of coulees from Bozeman to Big Timber as the wide lanes peeled away time like pedals of an artichoke. As we laid glistening green pastures and mountains behind us the hours of wheels humming under a broad sky were tamped with individual thoughts: mine included the tick of years gone, birthday lists, hellos and goodbyes, photographs captured only in my mind, and what ifs.

That sort of ruminating can't pay the bills it excretes.

The woman in the pickup and I drove together in shotgun fashion, giving way and gaining ground, hearing lugged tires buzz, learning a distant familiarity as we took turns staring down the dinged chrome of each other's bumpers.

We acknowledged one another somewhere east of Billings beyond the punchy draft of the refineries. Our gas tanks needed filling so we rolled into stations at Hysham or Forsyth, and then found each other again in the bluffs by Miles City.

After that, she turned south toward Ekalaka. A breeze sifting through the cracks of open windows carried the pungency of sweet clover as the bigness of land absorbed the T100. Its trail was marked by a thin line of dust that became the sky. I kept on the interstate to Glendive.

A T100 is a long box Toyota with four-wheel drive and a bench seat. The shift lever is the divider between the person at the wheel and the one by the ditch-side window.

This series of pickup truck seems indigenous to

the West where you often see the model years after its discontinued production.'

Wyoming has them too, and the parts of eastern Washington where the people know what happens at the stockyards out by the airport and don't care.

Not much, not often.

Thirty years ago it was all Ford and Chevy.

Dodge kicked its way into the major market with its bighorn sheep brand that caught the fancy of people with gun racks who were tired of the other two makes of junk coming out of the motor city. Maybe there's something to this Western motif, they groused, and threw in.

Out here on the slanted roof of the continent it was always pickups, and payload was a word that meant the same as, "How much room you got?"

From the eastern front of the Rockies to the Columbia sage flats, the number of bales that fit in a pickup truck bed, the strength of shocks and springs that kept the load, pulling power and whether you could haul the ewes with the tools and coolers to the sale or back with relative ease and in comfort, was more important than gas mileage.

Size mattered, bells, whistles and fuel economy didn't.

Back then, you wouldn't see a Japanese mockup of a pickup truck anywhere near a roping horse.

Who knows what changed. Toyotas made in Indiana, a state that fancied itself more sanguine than the puffed-up, union-owned conglomerates that passed on self-reliance, started to take hold in a meat and corn cob way.

23

Out west where oil rigs peck like emus against the horizon, the T100 caught the eyes of some in the buckaroo crowd feeling the pinch of paying through the nose at the pump and willing to sacrifice some payload for less maintenance. When the T100 added a bigger engine, it all made sense, at least for a while.

These Toyota trucks hauled grain and diesel, they were banged against by Hereford bulls and busted by beetle-killed pine when the wind blew wrong on firewood day.

You saw them now and then in town, usually on Sunday, and by their looks they had an AM radio tuned to gospel music or Mel Tillis, a good heater and room enough on the inside for the kids and a dog.

They usually wore dents like the dimple on the chin of Spartacus, and maybe that's what drew us to them.

We liked their look, but the make didn't last. T100s are an antique of sorts that we now slow down to regard.

The other day in Lewiston a red T100 with a bent tailgate was parked downtown and I made a couple passes and considered pulling over for a closer look.

I think these pickups may have done all right in Dakota, eastern Montana and the feedlots around Yakima, but hauling a real load up a mountain grade is not what they do best.

For that reason, the eight-cylinder Tundra eventually replaced the T100, and the people in Indiana, where the Tundra is made, do good work, I understand. The larger and more powerful truck has an engine with cylinders in V formation of geese heading north.

Its name, though, edges on pomp.

A jet and a lot of cash are required to get anywhere near the Brooks Range and once you're there, it's all backpackers in synthetic fabric eating energy bars wrinkling their noses at the Cummins diesels hauling pipe back and forth from the Slope.

No one in Hardin or Kinsey is enticed by the Tundra's vague nod to the vast and empty arctic with its wind-blown expanses and snow seen coming days away.

They have plenty of that without leaving their front steps.

Dodge's embrace of grit and endurance with its Ram worked. I see a lot of the full-curl, chrome, sheep emblems — agnostics say it resembles a uterus — on the road these days.

They haul loads. Uphill much of the time.

The T100 is a throwback. It revels on the endless road from hay field to sky and back and looks best with a buffalo head license plate bolted to a bent bumper. Reliable as ranch oats, this pickup may not have the muscle of its competitors but it's gangly, plenty tough, and good looking too. And there are a lot of them around. Even after all these years.

TANK CREEK

Finn the Boy His River

ST. REGIS — What does a kid see when he sees a fish?

He is five and enamored with trout.

He follows me to the river talking the whole way.

He will not stop talking.

I am a good boy, he says, I am almost grown up.

We drive the interstate to Montana, just he and I, and it's morning.

He cried at first because of the hour. He hadn't rubbed the

sleep from his eyes when I stood over him and said, Buddy, let's go.

His normal ritual includes his mother, but today it was too harshly a man thing, and the streetlights were still throwing umber on the sidewalk and dew, like split shot sinkers, tipped the grass.

"Trout like lots of ants and grasshoppers and 'caditz' flies, huh, Dad?" he quizzled. "They sit on the bottom and when a bug floats by, they swim up to eat it."

He sat by the front door with shoes in his hands and the big newness of heading off in the dark to a fishing hole hit him ruefully like a bowl of Jello salad.

He needs a hat, I said. And a sweatshirt.

In the car he pealed like a bell until I asked, what do you think they are biting on?

"Maybe ants," he said brushing away tears. "Winged ants."

We saw ants on the river last week, but used hoppers with some success.

Then, as we drove to the intersection, he straightened his back and explained the nuances of trout food.

I think it's fair to say that I am someone increasingly in need of a lesson from a five-year-old because fresh insight is a wire brush, and more often my mind is old paint.

"How far to the river?" he asked.

He napped and woke up somewhere on the trail, the broad, engine-humming trail, four lanes wide and abuzz with small cars that cracked the whip on performance with a bit of pressure on their accelerators.

"How far to the river, Dad?"

We shimmied down Lookout Pass and leaned into the curves. He insisted he needed a bathroom, so we throttled down at St. Regis for overpriced meat sticks, a pack of nuts and cupcakes. And to pee.

I answer a call on my cell phone in the parking lot. When I turn, he is using the tire of a nearby pickup as a backstop to relieve himself as tourists from east of the Mississippi stroll past, raising an eyebrow. They observe our Idaho license plates, adding another misconception to their inventory.

Each time we're in the area, we visit the gas station and gift shop to tap on the glass tanks full of live, bent-nosed trout that will never taste the wild rivers where at least a few strands of their DNA were long ago spawned.

We peer at the fish in the tepid water.

"That's a big one huh, Dad?" he says.

As large as the ones we will catch today, I assure him, and he presses his face closer to the glass, imagining a thick colorful fish at the end of his line.

The fish in the tanks have grown since he saw them a few months ago, the boy insists.

They must be eating a lot of ants, he said.

"What fish is that?" he asks tapping the glass. "What are those?"

Rainbows, brown trout, brookies and cutties – because children prefer fish with names that don't remind them of scary movies and cutthroat, Idaho's state fish, is such a name.

"How far to the river?" he asked.

We try out the popguns in the toy section and leave the store heading south over the hard-pack gravel road that will remain hard-pack gravel because grizzly bears are more prone to cross hard-pack gravel than similarly hard-packed, but black, pavement, according to the people who talk with judges who rule on such matters. Thus, this road, one narrow sinew in a thousand square mile bit of mountains and woods, will not impede bear movement, according to the federal judge in nearby Missoula who has likely watched the same films of grizzlies chasing bicycles down the paved thoroughfares of our Rocky Mountain national parks, as the rest of us.

How far to the river?"

Once we cross the divide we're greeted with pavement on the Idaho side, and we sweep through the many downhill turns and hit the Gold Creek intersection where we hang a left and mosey toward Red Ives. In the first parking lot, empty this time of year, he tumbles from the door to view the water.

I retrieve a tote from the back of the car with the word "fishing" printed in block letters with a permanent marker and we scrounge inside it for gear. I pull out a single wading sandal and a hat from a fly shop in Montana that I had forgotten about.

I wheedle out a fly box stuffed with imitations of elk hair for wings on rusted hooks, and find spools of spider wire fishing line and a wool-headed sculpin pattern that a guy down the river insisted will catch bulls. I put these in the pocket of my fly fishing vest, shuffle into a pair of long underwear unused since last October, and throw on a fall fishing shirt. Donning waders, we spill down the bank to the cobbly shore and cast patiently toward a rock wall for the trout that aren't coming up.

"I want to catch a trout," he says.

A fish rises to look at the small boy with the big fly rod.

It slaps its tail and scoots back to the river bottom.

"Did you see that?" I ask.

He grins.

"They want me to catch them," he says.

There is wisdom in children with fly rods.

There is remorse too, and the inevitable sadness of hooking limbs with back casts again and again, of reeling line backwards and the mess it can bring, and hours of not catching anything.

And then, there's the water.

Its quietude and forgiveness bring gifts of mayflies, fat caddis and carapaces, podlets of moss and the flit and cry of water ouzels. Its freshets and round rocks are smoothed by elements and the kind of time we'll never really understand. Its trout rise like holograms, float for a moment for a bobbing fly too gaudy maybe for this autumn day, before dropping into the water column, seeking out their lie behind a stone or in a rocky furrow of the stream bed. And when a fish is hooked and played upstream, the boy with a cap like a Little League pitcher, reels his own line quickly and jumps from rock to rock waving his fly rod like a guidon.

I'm over here, he calls. Wait for me.

Can I touch it?

Wait for me, he says. I'm over here.

Can I hold it?

He scrambles with a fly rod in one hand and hops over obstacles with the exuberance of a kid goat testing its legs in a high mountain meadow.

Can I kiss it for good luck?

He strokes it with a finger.

"Its eyes are big," he says.

"Is it a cuttie?" he asks.

He holds the cutthroat trout until it squirms and splooshes back into the current.

"He wants to swim," he says.

He watches it slip into the black, fast-moving water.

We head up the bank and in a pocket of rocks near the trail he finds a winged bug that is dead, cups it in his hands to show it.

"See," he says. "It's an ant with wings. I bet the trout eat that." At the next spot a mile downstream, he stands on a rock alone, casting.

"I want to catch a fish," he says. And he will.

When he does, it will be his fish.

In the meantime he waits for me to hook a trout so he can reel in his line, hold his fly rod in one hand as he bounds over to me, glancing off rocks.

"You do the easy part, and I'll do the hard part," he says, meaning he will reel in the fish.

What does he see when he sees a wild trout, and briefly holds it? What is he learning in such a native place, from such a free and wild river?

Hunting

Turkey Day Roadkill

It's the first snow.

We learned of its coming yesterday when the chimney smoke disappeared into a sky the color of a work shirt and the temperature hovered between pucker up and goose pimples.

Just in time for the holidays.

The next morning before daylight, pickup tracks from neighbors heading to work cut the fresh snow on the gravel road like a travois.

I follow them down the mountain and round a corner under a sky like black licorice when I meet a rig coming my way.

I veer right. The driver of the other vehicle, a homely dually with flopping fenders, doesn't bother tugging at the wheel.

A cigarette glows in the cab and three figures hunch shoulder to shoulder inside. I can almost smell the stale beer from last night's honk at the tonks and the acrid smoke from the Parker and Simpsons.

The men have rifles between their legs.

Right around Thanksgiving, the whitetailed bucks are crazy chasing does. The antlered sex of the species is high on testosterone and fermented fruit, oblivious to dangers that include rifle barrels steadied on the half open windows of cars or pickup trucks idling in a turnout.

This particular pickup uses much of my lane and I see the three-toned Chevy in my rearview swerve in the snowy muck before it taps its brake lights and disappears around the bend.

Smoke from its exhaust plumes oily as kerosene.

It is road hunting time in the peckerwood hollers.

At the game stations biologists measure tines and check teeth to age bucks killed after the first snow.

A man topped with a camo do-rag and sweat on his upper lip hasn't slept much, he says.

"Gotta get out early before the yahoos hit the woods," he laments to a slight woman with game department patches on the shoulders of her jacket and a tape measure in her hands.

The buck the man displays is a five-by-five with antler bases big as bananas. It still has that effervescent glow in its eyes as if it died ruminating the origins of a spotlight.

Big bucks come and go, so do poachers.

The first snow makes hunters slap happy and after that, sky's the limit.

A sport shop in town shows Polaroids of all the big deer taken by whatever means since Elvis slept at Graceland.

"Where's yours?" asks the woman behind the counter.

She's quick as a switch and twice as sharp.

I'm fondling a photo of a thick-necked bruiser with antlers like a coat of arms and look up to meet her gaze.

"He shot that one from across a canyon in another time zone," she says.

"Nosler bullets," she says. "Faster than the speed of light."

She smirks.

"Yeah, right," she adds, as an afterthought.

Up in the hills, I round another turn and more headlights blind me. I slow my small Japanese-model pickup and pull over for a behemoth as wide as a motor home. It churns by bedecked with hunting stickers, as its high beams light the forest like a July wildfire.

The truck is a tugboat spoiling a wake. Inside there's a heat-seeking cannon and a man with a Pepsi. He wears all-day boots, fleece camouflage jacket and pants, and his heater is a ten thousand BTU flame thrower.

He had a chance at an apple-fed deer at the orchards a mile back without knowing it. The trees there drop fruit on the road and the bank is covered with snow. Plug a feeding deer and you can slide it from the bank into your bed like at the Get-n-Go.

But his CD player thumps rock and roll so loud the deer heard it coming an hour ago.

Let's face it, I've road hunted too, and been party to grinding gears to get a deer.

The sound of distance when I hunt, is preferable. Or, no sound at all except the snap of twigs or the huff in the brush from an invisible buck that scents you.

Up on the Gulch where I live there are hunting spots with names like "the point field," "the scrape line," "gitters middle" and "the sisters."

There's "the canyon," the "breaks," and "big brush" where elk often hole up this time of year.

Neighbors who have lived on the Gulch since the forgettable Jimmy Carter years remember how no one ever traveled up there.

"Three cars a week and we'd walk outside to watch them pass," said Doc, who raises Targhee sheep up the road from me. "It was like TV."

His family and a very few others had the run of the place and filled all their deer tags by turkey day and when March rolled around, they drank water through a straw on account of the six-month's worth of tallow caked in their craws.

That's what Doc said.

Hunting, despite the waning numbers nationwide – a ten percent drop from over fourteen million a decade ago to twelve million today if you believe the newspapers – remains popular on the Gulch and similar rural holdouts.

Road hunting, especially.

I once steadied my .257 over the hood and knocked a four-point buck off a side-hill on Thanksgiving Day. After the successful undertaking, I tip-toed through the road mud and up a wet bank in a painfully arduous attempt to retreive the deer and hoist it into the bed of my pickup without soiling my church clothes.

Fortune had me bring a change of shoes.

One morning on the way down the Gulch to the children's daycare center my four-year-old daughter, who had developed a taste for venison, yelled "Daddy, daddy, there's a deer! Shoot it!"

We don't shoot deer from the road, I told her, but it was a lie.

You shouldn't, I would tell her now.

But there are times when you must.

TANK CREEK

Heaven and Tamarack

How close do you want to get?

Close enough to touch it, he said.

Heaven can be interpreted in a number of ways. Blue jeans, a tank top and a sweating bottle of cerveza in the shade of a buccaneer palm while leaning on the fender of a '68 Firebird is among them.

This, however, wasn't that.

On this particular day we were attired in cargo slacks with a northern forest motif. The cuffs had a string that allowed tightening over the tops of our Gore-tex lined boots, and our shirts and jackets were a perfect accretion of camouflage so that standing next to a trail winding through an overgrown logging clearcut with our faces painted like Gurkhas, the only thing that showed was our teeth.

"I can't stop grinning when I'm out here," he said.

We leaned forward on an elk trail trodding, one step at a time, through mountain clearings planted long ago with

41

tamarack and fir that barely crowned our heads. We stepped through the jagged forests that edged the logging like picture frames, and crossed gated haul roads.

It was the season when the leaves fall from the trees.

We knew this because glancing through the timber, a yellow, plate-size cottonwood leaf on an otherwise barren tree invariably waved from a limb causing us to raise the binoculars, anticipating the back end of an elk.

"That's just a leaf wagging."

"I see that."

"No cause for alarm."

"I'm not alarmed."

And so on.

We had earlier hiked through a forest to a gravel road. At its edge a vine maple, a knotted rope of a sprite, had shed its flaming leaves. They splattered on the rain-wet dirt like a cut artery making a homicide of the road bed. Standing among the circle of crimson and cardinal shades stamped sacrificially to mud, the bell-like fount tested our regard for the divine.

"Wow. Lookit this."

"Who tipped the pomegranate truck?"

"Jesus, that's who."

It was clearly a sign of celestial artistry, the sanctity of nature and its genius to create. This example of expiration was proof of an animated and existent paradise.

We had climbed out of Lost Girl Creek in the early rain, through the clearcuts like a pack train except it was just the two of us, not saying much. We breathed hard, exhaling the pressure we felt in our lungs. We were human mules in damp clothing and boots with welts that stuck and didn't slip depending on the determination behind each toe kick.

Sometimes we stopped just for the view that shimmered under low clouds brushing the tops of trees.

We looked at our rifles and marveled at their weight.

Eight pounds plus the cartridges.

A one-pound rifle scope.

The firearms we carried were without a sling because we decided when we were much younger that swivels squeaked, potentially scaring game. Therefore we developed a habit of lugging our rifles — on the ready — in the crook of an arm, bearing the burden like Episcopalians.

The rest of the ballast was part of the business of climbing in and out of places we deemed occupied by the animals we were after.

Our boots, wet at least on the outside, were several pounds apiece and a filled water bottle weighed almost a pound. We each carried three.

Other items befitting our characters included a woolen railroader vest with six brass snaps. A seven-ounce folding knife. A sheath knife with a heat-treated blade, its aluminum pommel guard and phenolic handle added weight we didn't feel.

One of us carried a sidearm that weighed two pounds, and added three ounces for the cartridges.

Binoculars weighed thirty ounces.

In our backpacks we hauled meat bags, a flashlight, rope, fire starter and candles.

We wore double-layered undershirts with long sleeves and waffle thermal bottoms with woolen socks and carried along extra this-and-thats, the sort of fundamentals your mother would require, including a set of dry undergarments rolled tight and plastic bagged.

Humping uphill on a trail spotted with elk and deer tracks through a day determined to break clear-skied, we tended individual thoughts.

There is a story behind place names and the general area we hiked was given its moniker when local streams, at the time of Wyatt Earp's escapades into the Idaho Panhandle, were alive with mining ventures.

Families were staked miles from tent towns as pap humped to and from civilization with his poke, carrying back to the family in a tar paper shack the grub, tools and necessities for a comfortless life on the claim.

A young girl was lost out there where mountain streams flowed together, and she was not found despite the week-long efforts of search parties.

The place came alive when groups of men and women of many dialects — Gaelic, Slaski, Frisian and Swiss — neighbors from miles around drummed from hogsback to bottomland, crossed streams and canyons calling the child's name.

The girl's dog, a small spaniel, whimpered back to camp but the girl did not return.

A dearth of favorable news, or any sign at all of the child eventually drove the family to madness.

Grief stricken and hampered by an inalienable sorrow of a life scratched so far from home, mother, father and siblings pulled up stakes and returned to Pennsylvania, while miners for years left the place alone.

They were certain they heard the girl crying, or calling out on windless days in a small, singsong Piedmontese near the place where a host of streams entwined.

A century and more later, through a country mostly tamed, we followed the creek named for the missing child, keeping to a high bank where the elk left a furrow as they kicked uphill.

We followed this trail into the brushless dark of high canopies. Following, as it gained elevation seeking pockets of light. We followed the tracks out of the mist and into the edge of clearcuts, wide open places of sky and low clouds with their slopes replanted with seedlings. Climbing through strips of standing timber along the stream, we dipped our heads to the fanning arms of cedar, were slapped by leaves of hawthorn and currant and entered another clearcut.

This wide open, flourishing forest of miniature trees, tamarack mostly, was golden with small green firs that grew to the tops of our hats. Some of the trees towered higher, rising seven or eight feet, and through them wound the elk trail.

Additional trails like tributaries fanned away from the main route and rejoined it.

A caterpillar tractor, more recently, had cut a swath

through the standing new growth and this steep road was grass covered and painted now with the fallen yellow and orange needles of the larches.

Nearby was another chunk of standing timber, a quarter section, give or take, and when we breached it we found the road with the ruby leaves of the maple.

In another clearcut, higher up, we sat on stumps surrounded by a burnished blanket shaggy as a herd of Highland cattle.

We looked uphill and marveled.

There was no overt sound just a breeze that stopped and started, prompting the tinkling of tamarack needles as they fell from the trees. We felt wonderfully isolated from the humanity we had sought to escape.

The impression made him grin.

"This is it, isn't it?" he said. "This is pure heaven."

From far away and over a mountain came a buzz from a single engine plane we couldn't see. Its vibration through clear air reinforced the sense of distance we had put between us and mechanical things.

A slew of elk tracks from animals that had gathered here, likely this morning, gave us promise.

The fragrance of a wallow maybe, or single animals fringing a small herd, floated on a breeze.

Nodding to each other when the draft was right, we inhaled the pungency that pierced an already sweet-smelling morning.

We picked up our gear and hiked higher into the sea of small, golden larches until we stepped through the ceiling of fog and stopped on a bench with a view of the surrounding dips and swales that, like a cupped hand, encircled us. The sky broke blue and then white like an eye.

"We're here," he said. "We're in God's pocket."

We leaned our rifles against low limbs and raised our binoculars as the mist burned away.

"Gunslingers in paradise."

It was early, not yet midmorning.

"C'mon mister elk," he said, glassing the hills.

"This is where I want to stay," he said. "With just enough earth to embrace."

It was heaven alright and we had humped hard to get here.

The glint of an antler, the dark ruff of a neck or the yellow rump of wapiti blending into the hillsides; the flick of an ear, or thundering hooves would be frosting.

"I can't stop from grinning," he said.

TANK CREEK

Boats, Autumn, Rivermen

SPRINGSTON — If you motor up the Coeur d'Alene River from the lake it is best, if you're a novice, to do it in early summer before the coontail, parrot feather and pondweed curls like maidenhair near the topwater, constricting the channel and choking the boat's propeller.

The late-season channel isn't a bother to jet boaters who are heard miles away, gliding over the lake on mirror-flat mornings like high octane water skimmers.

The workers at Harrison Dock Builders are well versed in the river's ins and outs because their headquarters, moorage, and paycheck are a mile upstream, so follow them.

Being on a river in a boat is a lot of what North Idahoans take for granted. The rivers here have always been working rivers. The Coeur d'Alenes used them for navigation, their wildlife for sustenance, placing fish traps inside channels, carving bones to hook the river's trout and salmon.

Settlers floated logs on the St. Joe and Coeur d'Alene rivers

All that remains of The Golden Star, a former steamer that was beached in 1955 at Springston.

and as the population of newcomers grew, the waterways became liquid highways for passenger steamers, tugboats and rafts of harvested trees heading for the sawmills from St. Joe City to Post Falls.

Decades ago, even as late as the 1990s the men who piloted the steamers that worked the rivers, towing logs and hauling material to St. Maries, Springston and Winton could talk of the olden days on the water. But the bulk of the skippers are gone and what is left are the pieces we remember of their stories.

Few visible remains tell what landmarks guided these men, and what challenges they leaned against. Little is left to provide a tactile knowledge of the boats they steered. Unlike steel wheels rusting in Midwestern fields, or busted windmills with faded names of agricultural companies mired in dirt surrounded by wheat, the steam-powered boats that worked the rivers have vanished into the maw of time.

Sleek watercraft with names like Pine Cat and Flyer are captured only in museum photographs. Many of the vessels were burned to the hull and drowned off some rocky point in deep water where scuba divers glimpse the remains through bubbles of expelled air.

Unlike the railroad cars propped next to fish ponds for travelers to ponder, or bucket chains and headstalls from another era displayed alongside information signs in mining country, the tugs and boats fueled by steam from boiled water live mostly in our imagination.

What did the old skippers say?

Gil Roe was ninety-something, residing in a Hayden,

Idaho, mobile home park behind an iconic burger joint and its lumberjack billboard, when he recounted his time as a younger man working the waterways of North Idaho. He was born in Harrison, attended school in Conkling Park and as a teenager was launched into the world of steamers, logs and river drives.

"I started out in 1925 as a lineman on the St. Joe Boom Company steam tugs," said Roe, his clear voice trailing a direct gaze like a wake from a vessel's prow.

"I operated most of them," he said.

The Pine Cat was a tugboat owned by Lafferty Transportation Company, one of northern Idaho's premier towing companies. Lafferty Transportation pulled logs on the Shadowy St. Joe River from 1918 until the 1970s when the outfit was sold.

The Cougar, another boat Roe piloted, was known seventy-five years ago as the cream of the northern Idaho steam-powered tugboat crop. Roe operated the St. Joe too, and the St. Maries, towing logs to mills mostly from lumber operations in the St. Joe River drainage.

The timber sticks were stamped like doggies with the branding hammers of logging companies and hauled from the mountains on trucks with water-cooled brakes to landings along the river. Log loads were dumped into the current and when the bobbing wood reached a slower-moving river downstream, the logs were corralled and sorted by tugboat men and their crews.

The rafts, called brails, were towed from places such as St.

Joe City and Ramsdell on the St. Joe River below St. Maries, to Beedle Point at the southern end of Lake Coeur d'Alene, a trip of more than twenty-four hours.

From there, they were pulled, lethargically, another forty-eight hours to sawmills at the north end of the lake around the city of Coeur d'Alene and Post Falls.

These days, houses and the docks of the well-to-do have replaced the mill buildings that tempered the garish growl of the band and circular saws. A new industry has risen from the brownfields of former mill sites offering leisure and prime real estate where once the work had been.

"You take in them early days," Roe said. "They would drive two hundred million board feet of timber out of Marble Creek and float them free, and the company would take them downriver from slack water."

On the St. Joe River, slack water began thirteen miles upstream from St. Maries at Ferrell where the St. Joe Boom Company stored bunches of its logs. The town is gone now, alive only in the memories of people like Roe.

A variety of jobs were available to those who wanted the work. Required was grit, savvy to sidestep the dangers, and a cat's balance to walk on floating logs with a large pronged pole — called a pike pole — used to push or pull logs and retrieve line, or later, the wire rope "swifters" that secured the logs.

It was Roe's first job.

"It was caulk shoe work," he said.

Men wore nail-soled boots to keep from losing their

footing. They stayed on the logs as they were towed downriver, using the pike poles to ensure the logs didn't snag on river banks or sand bars, or slip from the brails.

Lunchtime wasn't spent on the tow. For the men on the brails, the tugboat could only be reached by a tightrope walk on the towline.

"When noon came and lunch was ready, why, you either walked that, or you stayed back there," Roe said. "But you had a pike pole that you balanced yourself with. The pike poles were about ten or twelve feet long. We would shimmy up them ropes and think nothing of it."

Hap Murphy was a former skipper too, who towed logs on the St. Joe River for almost two decades before the Second World War.

"It was the most beautiful place on earth," he said, thinking back at ninety years old.

Although the St. Joe still hints at its earlier beauty, in reality, Murphy said, the river now is just a shadow of the paradise he knew.

Motorboat traffic and water backed up by a hydropower dam have eroded its banks causing the once magnanimous cottonwoods at Chatcolet Lake to topple into the current, discoloring it with the mud made from dirt the trees' roots dislodge when they fall.

"It's all one big puddle," he said. "It breaks my heart to go up the St. Joe River now."

There was a time, though, when a younger Hap Murphy spent his days, and many nights, piloting fifty-foot steam tugs and diesel-powered boats around the bends of the Shadowy Joe.

"The steamboats were wooden boats," he said. "They had twelve-gauge iron on them so they could go through the ice."

When the ice got too thick — about eighteen inches — work ceased for a season.

But it is the summer and fall on the slack water of the St. Joe River that Murphy recalled with a fondness of one who once knew the bends and sandbars in his sleep.

"In the fall, the fog would rise off the water and the sun would break through like opening a door or something," he said.

Idle your boat up or down the St. Joe in the early morning, especially in autumn, you will see what Murphy was thinking.

The river is lonely for the most part and, a while back, floating a skiff through the mist, I slipped in among a cow and bull moose feeding along a bank near the channel at Benewah Lake. The animals displayed a slow ethereal grace that eons of genetics had ingrained. I might have been in a pirogue dripping water from a paddle.

Earlier, on a summer morning, I motored up the Coeur d'Alene River to the Springston bridge and floated just long enough to watch the rising sun tip through the cottonwoods and flicker on the shell of a boat on the bank.

Glenn Addington, the former mayor of Harrison, a lifer of the lake and its rivers had a particular grace when speaking of the olden times. Addington was also a skipper of the steamers and it was the boat he ran aground on the banks of the Coeur d'Alene River at Springston that is remembered by those who visit the place.

To many who see it, the Golden Star appears to be grounded by mishap, or a feat of malfeasance. Its wooden skeleton — more of it remained a couple of decades ago — was carved into the sandy bank under the steel bridge where the community of Springston once sprawled around a sawmill, which is gone too.

Some of the area's history can be unlocked behind the door of the Harrison museum.

Addington's account of steamboats and in particular the one he beached on the bank of the river in 1955 after piloting her for eighteen years, pulling log brails on the St. Joe and Coeur d'Alene Rivers, can be read in a newspaper from 1981.

"There was always an oily, steamy, hot smell," Addington told the Spokesman-Review. "I can still smell it … You never get cold on a steamboat."

The Golden Star was sixty-three feet long, fourteen feet wide, and drew seven and a half feet of water. It was built in 1937 for the Russell and Pugh Lumber Company at Springston by a man named Andrew Knudson. He had a reputation for "building his boats with a hatchet." The marks from the blade could be seen on the hull of the beached vessel before they weathered away.

The Golden Star was converted to diesel in 1945 and its steam engine was used in the Springston mill to run a conveyor belt, a fate that Addington compared to "putting a racehorse out to pasture."

"Steam is different than diesel," he said. "You take the energy from the water, from the lake. You pump it into a boiler, build a little fire under it and you have energy. Can you beat that?"

And the only sound a steamer made was a breath-like huffing in the stack, and the melodic rhythm of the pistons.

"The water was free. All you had to do was convert it to steam," he said.

He recalled nights along the river when he tied up to the bank under the stars and the only sounds were the quiet heartbeat of the steam engine, the hum of swarming bugs and fish rising for them.

At seventy four, Addington lamented not having jerked the old steamboat off the shore, tied it to a couple of cedar logs, and floated it to Harrison where it could have been made a showpiece like those tractors, headstalls and trains at roadside attractions, instead of letting her rot on the riverbank.

After so many years underfoot, rocking him to sleep, and churning him awake, he still felt an attachment to the steamboats and their machinery.

When a person becomes accustomed to steam-power pushing a hull, and the engine and its vessel adapt to the person, the two become one thing, Addington said.

"It's like an extension of your body," he said. "You get so you have a sense about how far you can go with it. You develop a sixth sense."

TANK CREEK

The Whole Day

In Avery, Scheffy wears a white T-shirt and joggers with his feet pressed into a pair of bathroom slippers as he entertains two men who spent the morning spincasting in a fork of the upper river.

The sky is gray outside his store on a former railroad siding that now makes up the highway and a few staid city streets.

Temperatures are pleasant for October and despite the clouds that hide the ridges and press against the treetops, it doesn't feel like rain.

The men sit heavily on ratty-top stools in Scheffy's store cradling a twelve-pack of light beer they haven't paid for yet, mulling the day.

"Can I interest you in a few sausages to go with those," Scheffy smiles, nodding toward the machine with the stainless steel wheel on which sausages and hot dogs rise and lower in a small, heated chamber behind a glass door.

"I dunno," one of the men grumps. "What do you say, Harry, you want a dog?"

The suspense, like churning butter, is immutable.

I walk outside and look both ways down the long, empty forest highway — once the Milwaukee line's railroad right of way — that follows the river, then cross the pavement to visit Dan Mottern at his fly shop across the street.

The lacquered wooden sign with the carved trout that advertises his Idaho Fly Fishing Company has been taken down for winter.

A forgotten aluminum ladder leans against the cross members on the two, tall posts where the sign was.

When I walk through the door of the fly shop I am met with an unusual emptiness. The banter of tourists, hands stroking fly rods and wooden nets, the sound of streamers picked with tweezers and dropped into plastic cups, children screeching for ice cream and the clicking of a dog's feet on the wooden floor like cyclical blips of an electrocardiogram have been replaced by quiet.

A sullen light falls through the windows.

Dan's wife, Beth, appears from the back of the shop.

He isn't here, she says. He's gone looking for elk.

She makes me a triple shot Americano and says it's on the house.

"Wonderful," I say.

The river froze last week, Beth says. Edges of glass and fraggle ice could be heard crackling from a mile away.

It was amazing.

"The whole valley sounded like tinkling bells," she says.

I carry my coffee outside and listen to the silence.

Jim Surley who lives a few places upstream is gone too, but the banner that tells of his sentiments when it comes to the wolves the government introduced into the state is tacked to a wood pile facing the highway.

Surley, a former Army Ranger from another era, is probably in a draw somewhere, loaded for canis lupus.

I'm playing hooky from obligations today. It's the first time in months I got up in the dark, loaded the car trunk, and just drove away.

I meander upriver passing haunts where summers ago friends and I stopped to take in scenery, to watch with a kind of muted exuberance as bugs tumbled from the water or into it. Where we spied trout tails swirling the translucent green, or just watched each other as the sun dropped like a pinjata while we wriggled into still-wet waders, or out of them. Tying fishing knots or clipping line, sipping longnecks with arms and faces tanned, rain scarred or drowsy from a day casting and securing footholds on slippery rocks.

Those places are without fishermen today. Aside from the flowing water, the entire valley seems motionless. It betrays a solemnity that nudges distance and time. It whiffs of nostalgia, but the aroma is stippled with the scent of fir, cold water, the autumnal fervency of hunting and gathering.

It's a sentiment that says, you're on your own and be grateful about it.

I stop not far above the Upper Landing and nose the

Oldsmobile into a guard rail, crack the trunk and start the
ritual of dressing for the task at hand. I scold myself for
leaving the long underwear in another tote in the trunk of
another vehicle. I pull on a pair of stockingfoot waders and
stuff the tails of my sweatshirt inside. My wool cap is an
official Seattle Seahawks booster hat. My wading shoes are
ones I retired a few years ago, but felt compelled to dig again
from the woodshed.

"These'll do."

Alongside the road that disappears far off like a vapor trail,
there is a rod to assemble, line to thread and a leader to mend
before getting to the heart of the matter.

A dry or wet fly? A bead head or a high-floating top
water bug?

Cow elk season is over, so most of the camps have cleared
out, their hunters headed home days ago.

This is the solitary season. Not even the engine brake
of a logging truck cuts the quiet. Just gray overcast with
infrequent flashes of autumn sunlight blinking on the moving
water and disappearing.

I drive farther upstream, stop the car and get out. The river
narrows and moves heavily through a chute below me, but
on the far side a shaft of water bumps against a rock before
tailing into a soft fan that is sucked into the main current.

I know this place from summer, but it fishes better in October.

Near a rock like a globe of gneiss, a cutthroat sips the
surface furtively in long pauses away from the miasma of the
main channel.

The bigger than average fish rises and its body flashes like old ivory under the water's surface. It sips and turns full profile showing the red along its pectoral fins. The feeding trout barely dimples the surface before returning to its hide on the stony river's bottom.

From where I stand on the opposite bank it would take a hard cast and a big mend, followed by a very short float, before the current between here and there stretches the line and drags the fly unnaturally, scaring the fish.

A cast that bellies the line upstream may be a better bet for a short presentation.

The steep road bank is flecked with dead thistles, elderberry and brown knapweed.

I shuffle down the riprap to the river, find a boulder to stand on and cast first upstream.

I lengthen the cast and snag the bank behind me, hooking the knapweed by the guard rail. Dropping my rod, I bound up the bank to unsnarl the fly. I lasso a limb of elderberry on a cross cast, break my tippet and fear my rod tip has snapped.

It would be the third fly rod tip in as many years that has succumbed to falls or bad timing.

Tying on a smoke-colored stimulator, I take stock.

This is how it works and why people say fly fishing is just another of life's mirrors.

You breathe.

You forget about the broken things.

You let your heartbeat mark time and focus on the endeavor at hand, count cadence, let distance and past fall away.

It is what Musashi called No-Thing-Ness.

You know what you know. The past is gone. Future is a moment away. Let your senses seize it. There's nothing to lose or gain that's in your power to lose or gain.

My next cast falls short. The fly lands on the far side of the current and I mend, once, then again, before a splash near the fly says fish, and my line draws tight.

I catch a fourteen-inch, red-sided trout and on the next cast another larger fish sloshes as if the river is made of gelatin, but I am unable to reach the ivory-colored feeder and decide to wade.

Slipping from the bank onto an underwater rock, I let myself sink into the river. I feel the cold current through the waders and the moving water heaves against me. My old boots are light and their felt soles stick to the strata. Their entire life has been spent on this river. Nosing toward the river's center, the weight of the water presses against my chest and wants to push me downstream. For a moment I fear it might crest my waders and pour inside like a spigot, but I push through a furrow and the river bottom begins to rise up and I feel like I'm climbing from an otherworldly abyss.

When I turn to face upstream I see the ivory fish slurp quietly.

I slip closer as the current swirls around me.

I wade directly downstream of the feeding trout, stop and breathe. Thirty feet away, I climb onto a rock like a casting platform and unhook the fly from a rod guide. The vantage allows for a better view. I pull cold-stiff fly line from the reel as gears smoothly spin.

The wings of the stonefly imitation are pressed tightly against the fly's body, so I flare the hackle with cold fingers.

I have one cast.

I know this.

Stepping onto the rock, balancing gingerly, gaining altitude, the river careens past my thighs.

One false cast upstream away from the place where the fish feeds, and then turning, I cast directly over the feeding trout.

I let the line spool out.

The fly drops into the water several feet upstream of where the fish lies but I cannot see it because of the glare of the gray sky that has turned the water into a silver sheet.

I watch what I think is my fly bobbing in the current that sweeps around the rock and before the trout takes the nugget I squint into the reflection of the sky on water. When I see a dimple I set the hook. I am not sure it is the right time, but I raise my rod tip and feel the fish there.

The rod stops and the line tightens and raises water from the sheet metal brightness throwing sparkles of spray.

The river's ripples are small uncut diamonds.

The cutthroat immediately dives deep into the black current bending my fly rod like a witching stick.

I nudge the fish from under what looks from this distance like a boulder and then the trout turns toward the main current, throbbing, pulling line from my reel in a steady and forceful drumbeat that tests my blood knot.

The knot holds as I ease the fish higher into the water column and away from the main flow.

I bring the fish closer and it tries again to go deep before turning upstream.

The line is cable taut and I lift the rod tip so it bends like a bell curve.

The fish's head breaches the surface before nosing down and under.

In a moment I have the cutthroat on top, then in my hand as we breathe.

It's gills flare. The current is cold as electricity.

I measure the fish's length against my rod – it is bigger than the others – and look in its eyes.

Yellow eyes like a bird, its body red sided and barely spotted.

That's a pure strain cutthroat, I hear a voice say. It is the voice of a man who spent most of his life on the river. He told me years ago that these fish, the ones sparsely spotted with red gill slits and marble eyes, are the ones whose genome was birthed in this river's tributaries, under its cut banks, in the gravely wash of its mountain water, and I have little cause to argue the point.

I unhook the hair fly from the fish's jaw and lower the trout into the cold current.

It's autumn and I have another twenty miles of river to fish before I turn back downstream and hit the holes I missed.

There is one place I know holds at least one large fish.

One spot I know for sure that has a trout as long as my forearm in the soft water along the bank.

It is the hole I drove all this way to visit.

I pick my way back across the river, pushing through the cold current, careful to keep its water from spilling into my waders. I crawl up the bank, cross the empty highway as my felt soles leave wet prints on the pavement.

I secure the fly rod under a windshield wiper.

There is no one else fishing and I've got the whole day.

TANK CREEK

Tank Creek

Skosh and Ulysses stand in the snowy driveway overlooking the river.

One of them is dour with the meaning of the thing.

The other, Skosh, who takes after his mother, not his dad, Ulysses, who is tall and thin, grins.

There has been a miscommunication.

Ulysses wants to load his side-by-side ATV onto the trailer attached to his pickup truck and take it to town, but Skosh needs the all-terrain buggy to retrieve his son who is hiking down a mountain looking for shed antlers and expects a ride before dark at a creek crossing up a road that is impassable with snow.

Only the tracked ATV can make the couple of miles to the rendezvous site.

It is March and daylight is no vendible commodity.

Ulysses, who wears a porkpie hat made of felt and a forester's jacket, wants to be out of Tank Creek by early afternoon.

"Or, thereabouts," he says, standing in the snow under two tall firs that provide shade in summer – today they block the view of snow-frosted mountains – mulling the predicament.

Skosh, who is dressed in an insulated flannel shirt and a ballcap takes me inside the cabin to show the shed antlers that were found over the weekend on a hillside across the river where both Skosh and Ulysses, long ago, hung a boilerplate of half inch steel cut with a torch.

The sheds he holds as he stands in the middle of the small cabin, well-heated by a firebox wood stove, are heavy whitetailed deer sheds, brown as a cedar shake.

Before their hike yesterday through the snow, and wending through deep tree-covered glades where animals often hole up this time of year, Skosh checked the steel plate that hangs between two posts in a clearing on the hill on the other side of the river and counted thirty two bullet dents.

They were silver smears of lead in the otherwise rust-coated surface of the boilerplate.

"It weighs a solid seventy five pounds," says Skosh, who often, when the river valley has cleared of tourists and even the locals are inside their well-insulated homes, rests a thirty-caliber bolt action on a sandbag and aims the barrel a couple feet over the target, tests the wind and pulls the trigger.

It had twenty dents before the hunting season, and since then he and his camp crew fired sixteen times from the sandbag rest on the picnic table under the meat pole and alongside the fire pit in the driveway.

"We had some rookies try," Skosh explains.

From fifteen hundred feet away, if there is little or no wind gusting up the canyon, you can hear the bullet plink a couple of seconds after it strikes the steel as the sound carries slowly back to the shooter seated at the wooden table with the rifle barrel resting on the sandbag.

"Hear it?" The shooter turns his head toward the others who stand around holding their breath lest they miss the quiet ping as if from a ball peen.

These men hunt and shoot like it's nobody's business.

The heavy target more than a quarter mile away keeps their aim true when an elk steps across a canyon, or a whitetailed buck angles down a hillside so far out you must use binoculars to count its antler tines. The experience makes the prospect of a killing shot less daunting.

"Almost looks like a solid five by five."

"I see crab claws on one side but no hangers."

"I should probably take it."

"Yeah, before it makes the brush."

Those shots require the skill that comes with practice, lots of it, and with the confidence that habit imparts.

Both Ulysses and Skosh, twenty five years difference in age, can hunt for days, sleep in the moss, crisscross the contour lines on a forest map and walk home dry, even in the rain.

Once, when neighbors threatened to call search and rescue because Ulysses had gone hunting out the back door and not returned for a couple of days, Skosh calmed them.

"Put the telephone down," he said.

"He always does this," Skosh said of his dad, who is seventy five and knows the country better than most.

Then he sat behind the steering wheel of his pickup truck and drove four miles up the river to find Ulysses walking downstream on the edge of the pavement with his rifle over a shoulder chewing on a strip of jerky.

"Think I can bum a ride?" the old man asked when Skosh slowed and rolled the window down.

"Doubt it," Skosh said. "I'm going the other way."

He drove on, turned around and took his dad to the cabin where Ulysses helped himself to stew.

"Slept at the edge of a cliff the other night," Ulysses said. "Lucky I didn't fall off. Had to walk all the way around the Sisters until I realized where I was. Been logged pretty heavy back there. Only saw a couple elk. Nothing too awful big."

Tank Creek is named for a draw where the railroad had a cistern and steam engines stopped to fill up when the train came from Chicago on its way to the coast.

The tank was a big contraption, overfull with water from the roaring stream sloshing and dribbling out the top. Partially built on scaffolding, part concrete and wood with steel rods for staves, some of the structure remains, moss furred, if you know where to look.

The rail line, called the Milwaukee Road, was built between 1906 and 1909 with more than six hundred and fifty miles of electrified track that carried freight and passenger trains including the steam-powered Hiawatha.

Before the line was abandoned in 1980, a teenage Skosh would sit on an angled perch above the tracks listening for the bugles of nearby elk that responded when the train whistles blew.

"We'd sit where dad put us, waiting for a train to roll through the tunnels and when it blew its whistle we held tight for a bugle and then chased it," he said. "We got a lot of bulls that way."

Ulysses was a logging manager for the forest service that once kept most of the timberlands in this river valley of eight hundred thousand acres that is rilled, riffed, folded, fault-blocked, fissured and cross checked by the workings of geological time. He has walked, dead reckoned and glassed a big chunk of the land over his thirty plus years in that occupation, and now he does it by memory and with a rifle much of the time.

He put his boys out to the woods when they were young, just as Skosh and Ulysses turn loose the youngest member of the family, a former college baseball pitcher, all of twenty years old. They drop him with a pack frame and canteens at the top of a drainage and let him go into the same up-and-down expanse of forest – fir, spruce, pine and tamarack – with its cougar, elk and bear, wolves and deer and rivulets, streams, black timber and bright sky. It is land veined steep and hard as a fist it will run you ragged unless you have the lungs of a lion and eyes clear for redemption because the country is an addiction like opioids. It steals your attention for anything other than the blood in your veins which allows tarrying out as far as the nutrients in your plasma will carry you.

A lot of boys never turn away from their obsession with this slanted country, its carnal seasons that gnaw at their psyche like a bag of promises offered to the willing.

They remain willing, until they no longer can.

Big Tom has lived on Tank Creek since he was injured doing pavement work and collected a payment, severance and state disability. He bought a couple of sweet acres overlooking the river on a terraced piece of pine, syringa and scrub alongside the dusty road not far from Skosh and Ulysses.

This was decades ago.

He built a house and shop and raised his children while carrying a running feud with the state game department over Canis lupus, the top-tier carnivore introduced into the mountainous jungle of the Gem State to appease the sensitivities of people with gym memberships and two-hour commutes.

The wolves eventually made a home in the rugged landscape behind his house where he hunted deer and elk. To reach his panhandle paradise, the wolves traveled three hundred miles of the roughest terrain in the lower forty eight. The wild dogs, singly or in groups, ventured from the site of the much-heralded release in a snagtooth corner of Idaho. Year after year they moved higher on the map, and horizontally too like tines on a rake.

Not long after the first dog howled from a timbered saddle where Big Tom kept a tree stand, the paucity of deer and elk became apparent.

The wolves were loosed according to a federal arrangement and were supposed to be managed locally after repopulation objectives were met. Endangered species status would be lifted, the government promised, once ten breeding pairs and a hundred wolves roamed the backcountry of the Snake and Salmon Rivers.

A decade later the number of wolves exceeded the objective by five hundred percent and individual packs marked territories in most of Idaho's 44 counties. Each occasion to abide by the federal decree was met with postponement. Court orders, gavel drops and injunctions were pushed by dark money environmental groups in Seattle, Portland, Boston, New York and Washington D.C. with an agenda no one wrote about in newspapers.

Reluctance to enforce the federal plan took into account no family or rural livelihood and no governmental responsibility. It ran up against common sense like an air bubble in a canning jar, and was the pleasure mostly of them whose urban wonderland was untouched by the scouring bristles of reality.

"I'll take you back behind my place," Tom told state wildlife officials at monthly get-to-know-your-neighbor breakfasts. "Where once were elk, all we see now is bones and wolf tracks."

His offer was left on the table like yesterday's truck stop special.

Tom and his family expected to fill a handful of elk and deer tags each year, but instead of roasts in the freezer, the uncut tags festered on the refrigerator door, unfolded under magnets, or matted like postage stamps inside leather billfolds.

"We live off wild meat," Tom grumbled to the officials. "It gets us through the winter."

Meanwhile the wolves gained momentum, their population continued to burgeon, and the active wolf packs soon permeated each corner and the entire state like syrup on a hot plate. It changed the dynamic, Tom said. The autumn soliloquy of bugling elk ceased, the untarnished blush of wild country became an experiment for the federal government.

Elk and deer pushed from the mountains by the predators stood knee deep in rivers in winter, anxiously eyeing the surrounding timber. They lurked at the edge of farm pastures or in forested strips along highways from which wolves shied. The tattered herds became vulnerable to barbed wire, trains and truck traffic. Sometimes they stayed on the blacktop, or ran down the middle of the pavement as if being chased by unseen dervishes. They bedded in apple orchards and stood warily in the shadows of barns.

"Fourteen elk killed in one night by a tractor trailer that plowed right through them," Tom said. "That sort of thing has not happened before."

Tom called the sheriff when his kids found a deer carcass lying partially eaten in a frozen blood puddle at the school bus stop.

"It wasn't there last evening," he said.

And when his wife stopped at an intersection a few miles downriver, a wolf circled her car like a domestic dog.

"At first, I thought it was a stray," she said.

Eventually, emboldened wolves seeking deer and elk that

stayed in the valleys ran down the unplowed river road in front of car headlights.

"We won't let our kids walk to the bus," Tom groused.

There was no end to the bitterness.

Big Tom petitioned the fish and game department to open a hunting season on the federally protected species. He considered the beasts to be part of a larger plot by faceless bureaucrats and monied elites with a desire to decimate the elk and deer herds and turn people off the land.

"We can't live here without hunting," Tom said. "Once there is nothing to hunt, the government will come for our guns, telling us we don't need them."

His and similar concerns of fellow Idahoans prompted a savvy commissioner to draw a wolf management plan that was presented to the governor, the attorney general and legislators. It reached the federal judge in Missoula, the unaudited environmental groups and their allies at the national newspapers.

By then, the extraordinary prosperity of wolves, their surge and phenomenal impact on deer and elk was mirrored in hunting reports. Entire herds disappeared and anyone hiking the backcountry documented the malaise: Skeletons of big, saber-antlered bulls, their bones picked, were found tangled in the hollows and bottoms of creeks with names like Whistling and Spotted Louie. Oily skulls with brown squiggle sutures, their mastoids popped, peppered the slopes of wintering grounds. Femurs were found bleached and cracked like candy, and once-fertile elk habitat was haplessly devoid of the big ungulates.

The commissioner's proposal included a full-on hunt of wolves in Idaho. On private property the season would not close, allowing owners of livestock to plug a wolf in their pasture during calving season without a federal inquiry or the looming threat of incarceration. It meant foregoing costly bench trials that dragged lethargically through years at taxpayer and the defendant's expense while the agrarian "perpetrators" kept planting and harvesting, crunching numbers to set the annual budget for their farms and ranches in an effort to forestall the threat of bankruptcy that the rational killing of one wolf had incited.

The commissioner's plan raised the neck hair on the money groups that attacked with the full force of their media partners. They poisoned discourse with half truths and more lawsuits that eventually, despite the greenbacks that paid for publicity, fizzled like the fort outside Missoula where many of the groups held court and where the district judge who had played the patsy for too long resided.

The acceptance of the plan and the removal of federal wolf protection was a victory for rural Idahoans. The decision was a win for the hunting and farming stock, the ones who spent their free time – away from laboring – recreating in Idaho's forests.

When the judge turned over the reins of wolf management to the state where it belonged, Big Tom, his face illuminated by the glow of the FM radio in the cab of his pickup, drove

the hour to town from Tank Creek to wait in the dark for
the doors to open at the bait and tackle shop. He planned to
purchase the state's first legal Idaho wolf hunting tag. When
the shop unlocked and Tom laid greenbacks on the counter,
he learned his was the first wolf tag sold in the county. By that
fresh hour, however, more than a thousand tags had already
been bought by the blue collar class in the southern half of
Idaho where commerce commenced an hour earlier.

The pavement starts on the other side of Tank Creek.

Miles down the road where it ends again and becomes a
gravel washboard Percy once bugled a chestnut-maned bull
elk from the back porch of the small house he built on the
banks of the river.

An elk herd often grazed in the moonlight across from
his big living room window, browsing ceanothus, willow and
dogwood on a slope that long ago had burned in a forest fire.

The elk silhouettes would first appear shadow-like until
the ridgeline was dotted with them. If you looked long enough
their rumps cashed the hillside like golden coins even at night.
Their sing-song canticles, cow and calf calls and whistling of
bulls, faded before morning sunlight slipped like an egg yolk
into the valley.

Percy rose from bed that full-moon night and standing in
the living room, he watched the animals on the hill before
waking his wife. He retrieved a bull bugle on a lark from
his sock drawer and walked outside to the porch where he
released a few squeals. The herd bull grazing the ridgeline

became suddenly frantic and loped all the way down the slope to the tangle brush. In the moonlight, it crossed the road and then stomped through the river before standing in the meadow near the porch intending to drub an unseen adversary.

Percy's wife, barefoot, wearing pajamas, slipping through the moonshadows on the dark side of the house, raised a carbine and opened the scope to let in light. She shot at the animal three times. Gunshots echoed off the walls of the surrounding valley but were muted by the trees and the rush of moving water.

"Shoot again," Percy advised after each muzzle blast flashed with no effect on the bull that craned its head and snorted mist into the night air.

His wife flipped the fallen strands of dark hair from her face and aimed again. The reports agitated the bull which seemed reluctant to retreat. It backed up a little when a shell was ejected, plinking and rolling around on the wooden decking. The uninjured bull crossed the river, then climbed back up the hill annoyed with Percy's continual haranging on the bugle and his wife's wild gunshots.

"She never even grazed it, I don't think," said Percy who twenty years later recalls how the valley has not changed much since that autumn. Similar opportunities to call a bull may still arise for others if they watch by moonlight, taking their chances with the game wardens who thoroughly frown at such misadventures.

With September's first frost scraped from pickup truck windows, curling white as shaved cheese on the hardened river gravel, Percy smells the steel air like he did those years when his kids were small. It is the same scent that curled through the cold brume on the night his wife missed the bull elk. He remembers the smell from his walks down the road to the five-room school house as a child. Same autumn smell. Same place. A different notch on the gauge of his existance.

His children, girls with red cheeks and pigtails, were raised along the river behind the short picket fence with a passel of brindley, long-eared Plott hounds.

The girls have grown to other lives in bigger places, but when the family was young, the daughters carried the fat-bellied Plott puppies like siblings. Red cheeked, they lifted the pups to peer over the whitewashed yard fence at passing logging trucks, at the timber-felling crew with its orange chainsaws and red Jerry jugs of saw gas. The girls waved with the puppy's paws.

Raised to chase mountain lions when days seemed green as a gooseberry, the Plotts were given names like Sadie and Bess, and they left this world as they introduced themselves to it, yelping, biting and fighting.

In a spring season with the snow waist deep, Percy's Plott hounds lay whimpering and dying in patches of bloody spoor in a mountain meadow overlooking the river not far from where the bull elk had raced down the hill to Percy's bugles a decade earlier.

The hounds had struck upon the scent of a lion and chased the cat sideways up the icy slope and over the lip of a ridge as Percy tried to keep up. It was the same lion that a pack of local wolves – the pack that had howled all winter from the tributaries near Percy's house – were, at that moment, harassing. The three Plott hounds, furious and hot on the trail, kicked snow and bellered directly into the group of wild dogs as if crashing a necktie party in the Queens basement of Robert's Lounge.

They immediately became the center of attention, outnumbered as they were.

A fight broke out that Percy, huffing until his heart banged a gong in his chest as he climbed the snowy trail, could hear, but not reach in time.

"Sadie and Bess were plumb dead," Percy recounted. "Robin, the best of them, she could walk down a cat in the meanest country, looked at me like she knew it was over. No throat to her. Rasping for air. I had to put her down."

Percy knocked one of the wild canids with a well-placed round from his .357 Cobra, a two-pound wheelgun he carried for such encounters, but the harvest, illegal at the time, was no recompense.

Up there on that hill overlooking the valley that early spring, the place where Percy had grown up and chose to scratch a living as a powder monkey, dump truck driver, gypo logger, cat skinner and lion chaser, another hardship was added to those that came before – and to the others, he surmised, that certainly would follow.

When Skosh returns from retrieving his son off the backside of the mountain, he buzzes up the snow covered pavement. The side-by-side's four-stroke engine screams almost siren-like in the distance. He returns to Tank Creek with elk antlers, a set of six pointers, newly shed with blood spoor in the pedicels strapped to the roof like sonar.

Ulysses anxiously paced the driveway in his son's absence watching the sky darken but unwilling to look at his wristwatch for fear the late hour would poison his nerves. His boot tracks snaked up and down the sloping path, milled where the road a half mile away downriver is visible through the standing trees.

The boot tracks now stop at the fire pit and the split fir, mostly embers with a few dancing flames, has been poked. Ulysses sits with the lug bottom of his soles facing the epicenter of heat, sipping a beer, when Skosh and the boy arrive.

"Looks like you found some good ones," Ulysses says, his voice quietly self conscious.

"All the way at the bottom, almost in the creek," the boy smiles. "I thought I would be skunked after three miles of walking."

Skosh drives the ATV onto the tilt trailer attached to Ulysses' truck and fastens the straps. The sky is pink as apple skin.

He lumbers over to the fire pit and stands looking at his dad who has dropped a chunk of fir into the flames.

"I thought you were raring to go," Skosh says while Ulysses stands now with one of the antlers beside him like a walking stick. It reaches almost to his arm pit.

"Kind of lippy aren't you?" the old man says, holding the beer bottle in his other hand as the brim of his porkpie hat tilts over an eyebrow.

He sets down the beer on the bricks of the fire ring and raises the antler with both hands examining the brown raspy bone and ivory spear tips. He nods approvingly before returning to his chair by the fire that pops and sparks.

"That highway ain't going nowhere," Ulysses says tipping his beer.

Snow

TANK CREEK

Lost And Found

He wasn't convinced the horns were stolen.

Not at first.

Then he found the back door to the shop ajar and the lock broken.

This man had hunted the same hillside since he moved to the edge of the county and built a small shop for his tractors and a modest barn for the livestock he kept.

When he took to the west side, and a new homestead below a timbered ridge bordering the state line, he thought his best hunting days were behind him. But mornings in the woods were something he had grown up with, so the idea of it pulled him back outside chasing horned animals mostly for meat, and sometimes for the prize of the antlers themselves.

The set of elk antlers that went missing were the largest and most beautiful he had procured in a life of killing big game.

This man wore a Western hat and a belt buckle the size of a wheel hub. His slim jeans gave him the appearance of a mantis, and each year for the past ten, he carried a .30-caliber rifle with iron sights to the eastern slope of a hill that curled and dropped into a creek bottom not far from his home.

He hunted elk and deer where the state had harvested the timber leaving broad strips of chunked up logs and debris from the mountain ridge to the lowlands. Grass, tall and bromey, grew up in bunches between shards of wood. Pockets of brush replaced the grass. Ceanothus and willow and berry vines attracted the animals he chose to hunt.

Gypo loggers cut more trees later on, so the place he hunted was in various stages of succession with scattered islands of timber, ground cover and browse. In the fall when the rain fell on the new tamarack that grew five feet high, the slim trees burst orange and yellow before dropping needles in the November wind.

The brush too, dogwood and sumac in shaggy patches, was gnawed and broken by moose, winter elk and whitetailed deer. In groves of uncut fir and pine, a hunter could hide from the wash of the rain as needle-matted ground was quietly dappled with water dripping from high limbs.

He drove his older model Ford pickup truck, red with silver panels, to the back side of the hill and climbed up a trail he knew well; one that others had not found, not yet, and quietly traversed the saddle. At morning's first light he sat down against the trunk of a thick ponderosa marked with blue paint that was left standing by the loggers because it grew on a southern aspect.

State foresters chose to harvest fir mostly on the slopes where ponderosas flourished, and the paint told loggers which trees to leave unmolested.

Fir was prone to burn while the western yellow pine with its thick, fire-resistant bark endured the flames that often kindled other species, allowing tongues of fire to dance in their crowns.

Digging the heels of his work boots into the duff, he waited for morning light to throw a silvery net over the clearcut.

He didn't hunt as often as many of his neighbors, but he was patient and diligently made the most of lighted hours during the few days each year at the same spot where he had killed a handful of small bull elk, and a couple of deer.

Sometimes he walked the timbered edges pacing himself.

Sometimes he waited for an hour near a swale that animals used as a trail.

"I find that if you just stay put, while everyone else is running around, you see more game," he told his neighbors.

"It sounds like you're just doing a lot of hiking with a gun," he often advised. And, "Open sights will keep you honest."

He might walk a mile or two, but the farther he got from his pickup, the more he realized how difficult it would be to haul out the meat from an animal he killed, and at his age distance was a limiting factor.

"I don't have those kind of legs no more," he said.

That is why the theft of these elk antlers, scored so late in his life, was particularly onerous and alarming.

It was no stretch to think someone would swipe those

horns, but an honest man who believed in the generosity of others might question such a thing could transpire. Others knew its likelihood.

After killing and butchering the elk with the six-point antlers that he shot on the hillside overlooking the carpet of tamaracks, making a short pack of the meat and carrying home the horns, letting them dry on a shop bench, this man drove to the coffee shop, showing the photograph.

"Beautiful ain't they?"

He displayed the picture at the fire department and showed it off at City Hall.

"Wanna see something pretty?" he said.

He adjusted his hat, rubbed a calloused hand over the brass of his belt buckle.

This was a town in which many people hunted much of the time whether or not the game department had an open season.

It was a place where people referred to elk and deer as their own, and where a hunter finding himself in the middle of a herd might shoot three, then call his friends on a cell phone to bark across farm fields in their ATVs like a roping crew to drag the animals out.

Trespassing signs didn't matter because it was mostly the newly-arrived whose appearance wasn't welcome who nailed neon orange signs to trees flaring the usual disputes about property lines, closed gates and barbed wire.

Precaution could have prevented the theft of his antlers. In a place where petty larceny next to misdemeanor trespassing was the top crime on law enforcement blotters, noone was immune to thievery. Similar transgressions fueled the felonies that often followed like a Morgan horse.

These antlers shouldn't be hard to find, the man told the police chief and the county deputy who patrolled the west side.

The elk rack was perfectly uniform, each beam a mirror image, he said.

He used a copy machine at the grocery store downtown to produce a small poster with a picture of the nut brown antlers with the matching six-point sides.

He displayed it at the hardware store. He stapled the poster to power poles next to photos of lost cats and dogs and fliers from the weight-loss groups, and he visited the school. The missing antlers may be the result of a high school prank, he told the superintendent. Be vigilant.

The poster showed a uniform set of walnut-colored elk antlers with daggers and evenly-forged stilettos for eye guards. They were neither heavy nor too light.

The fine set of bull-elk antlers drying European style on a cleanly whitened skull might have been the model for a picture on a coffee cup, or on the brochure of a refined hunting or shooting lodge.

He had planned to hook them over the sofa with framing wire like fine art. They would complement the plasma TV where he watched college football games and the Macy's parade.

When the man reported the burglary to the newspaper, its editor drove across the county, making the gravel road to the man's shop as the sun rose toward noon and the autumn air was cold as stainless steel. It smelled like snow.

The man with the calloused hands and big belt buckle showed the broken hasp, pushed aside the barn doors, and pointed at the empty workbench.

"They were settin' right there," he said.

A couple of neighbors were over for beers a few nights before, he explained.

They raved about the fine set of antlers and lavished praise on the man's hunting prowess.

One of them was a mechanic who worked on this man's Massey Ferguson tractor, and who had stuck a bull during the archery season, but it got away.

He was a good enough fellow, the man who lost his antlers said.

Drank too much.

"I got my suspicions," he said.

The bull he shot with his carbine with open sights had an arrow stuck into its rump like an antennae, he said. The shaft had worked its way into the bone.

The antlers weren't the only thing that was stolen, the man said.

"The arrow is gone too."

When confronted, the mechanic denied entering the shop and swiping the set of antlers. He seemed stunned, taken aback, and feigned offense.

"I don't need no more enemies," the man who shot the elk said.

"Them antlers shouldn't be hard to find," he said,

handing the editor one of the posters he made. "They are perfectly symmetric."

He likely wouldn't get another chance at such a fine bull, he confided. Not at his age.

"This loss has been a real hardship," he said.

TANK CREEK

Nine Degrees On the Last Day Of Pheasant Season

Nine degrees on the last day of pheasant season and the wind is a chafing blade of rusted steel against uncovered skin.

We have dropped from the road to a stand of aspen at the edge of a cattail swamp where, during the warmer season, the cover was home to salty birds hiding away from hunters who wanted dry feet. Most of the pheasant chasers in this crater of bottomland stay near the unirrigated agriculture fields leaving this swamp bowl with its border of pine and thorny brush in their rear views.

The dog and I parked on a gravel side road that was ice and snow-covered.

We collected our gear including a dog locator collar we call his hearing aid. Today in a world blazoned in white, the collar is non-essential.

The black-ticked dog and I crossed the main road and tumbled down a hill to the railroad grade and its brushy margins.

It seemed at first festive, the pointer and me on a fine winter's day.

A scathing wind, though, clashed with our enthusiasm. Its force lowered the mercury by a fistful of degrees as it swirled snow and pushed grainy ice in wavelets of silvery smoke into our faces.

Thinly-gloved hands took on a sharp numbness similar to the pain of getting whipped with a cord rope.

The twelve-gauge gun felt ponderous and the snow on the former railroad grade, sheltered from the prevailing wind by trees and occasional cut banks, was deeper than expected.

The dog was undeterred. He leaped from the railbank down to the brushy woods almost burying himself before popping out of the powder as if from a springboard. He jumped again, and again, catching scent on the wind as he burst forth from drifts that reached my thighs.

I followed, watching his tail spin as we zigzagged through the brushy jumble of lowland pines — a fine place for a pheasant to roost — without rousting a bird. We clamored up a hillside and down again through snarls of brush that offered patches of open ground, without spying any sign of harbored pheasants.

We hit the swamp, slushy under a couple feet of powder and not solidly frozen, and broke through its skin of insulated ice as we slogged on, leaving behind wet holes to mark our steps. The dog dove into whorls of cattail and rushes where I expected he would bust birds waiting out the storm, but no cackles followed, and no pheasants rose fluttering into the wind as we moved along the lee side of bluffs seeking protected swales.

The idea that brought us to this far-flung corner of country, as Robert Penn Warren might have it, was that gamebirds in this icy windstorm would likely hole up and stick tight. We planned to pick through overlooked pockets of cover where logic said the birds were fluffed and hunkered away from the draft.

Today, the last day of the season with the temperature a single digit, fellow hunters gave us nothing to grouse about because there were none.

No shiny or unshined pickup trucks from town were parked off the road with the Land Rovers or big-tire Jeeps that carried papered dogs in camo-covered kennels. Absent was the nod to the latest marketing trends that many earlier-season hunters evinced.

I marked one slick pickup truck idling along the county road as if considering birdy islands of snowbanked brush or grass. It pulled into a turnout across from a barbed wire-enclosed pasture a half mile away. Its engine hummed, and its cab heater likely ticked, as the driver considered the value of leaning into the whirling torrent with the cold barrel of a gun like a guidon while pushing through knee-deep snow with Fido. The pickup stayed a minute or two before speeding back in the direction it had come, as if eager for an MMA bout on the big screen and a tumbler of Proper Twelve.

This was the grind. The coarse grunt work of the bird season that despite its sense of fruitlessness, often provided unanticipated rewards.

Against our better judgment the dog and I moved into a windswept field and plowed through snow toward a grove of aspen a quarter mile away that looked promising, if the hardscrabble world of late-season birding held such a thing.

We followed a drainage ditch, cut a headwind through patches of scrub willow, and reached the strip of aspen where we recalled flushing birds a month earlier.

The place was barren now as an Andrew Wyeth winter scene.

We pushed through a swamp to an island of rushes that brought memories of a month earlier and one particular rooster that held tight before flying low, brushing the seed heads of tall grasses, as we held our fire and the dog briefly gave chase. That particular bird sank into the sedges unharmed and coasted out of sight, while today, no birds habited this place.

We edged into another pasture and halfway across, plodded toward a stretch of lowland brush that faded into bottomlands.

Having shouldered the draft, or turned our face away from it, we were relieved to find the gusts in this bowl of snow-covered pasture had somewhat abated.

We stopped.

The dog was first.

He stood motionless, belly deep in snow, then turned his head to watch me in what seemed a breezeless silence.

Thinking maybe he heard or smelled something, I put on the brakes and rested.

We had hiked almost two miles since leaving our starting point, had heaved through a landscape of white, brown and gray that showed no sign of a moving animal, nor did it offer a hint that any living thing had passed this way.

No tracks, no wild bird calls or sightings.

Wind-scalded, we listened to the quiet between the pulsing gusts on the other side of the ridge.

While the dog whirred and arced out front, I had come slowly, my gun cradled, then resting on a shoulder, or hanging from one hand in an effort to find a place with the least drain of energy.

In the hollow where we rested, the snow fell in sparse swirls.

On a high branch of a black cottonwood fifty yards away an eagle perched. The dog seemed to have noticed the scavenger bird and eyed it attentively.

We were motionless for different reasons.

For me, it was to breathe easy and take in the dull landscape devoid of scent or slivers of sound.

Seconds ticked.

The dog watched the eagle while his nose distinguished under-snow smells. He discriminated between near and far away, what is to be chased, chewed, or urinated upon, or best left alone.

The eagle preserved energy with its stillness under down-pressed coverts, surveying the distance for anything that meant food.

I whistled.

The eagle didn't move, but the dog pivoted his head.

"Let's go, Bud," I said.

We left the sentinel bird behind us and angled east through a thin finger of aspen, back over the ridge toward the pickup. We moved slower than before, heading toward the road and railroad bed that lay on the horizon like a shoreline.

As we peered across this expanse, we notice a man.

His dog, a white and umber pointer, came first, and my dog, Jack, was noticeably excited by the movement. The man's pointer hunted through a strip of wind-blown trees and grass we passed over a half hour earlier. An orange burst like a flashing strobe appeared behind the dog, then disappeared and reappeared before coming into view on a knoll. The man's orange vest was now easily visible and the man raised a hand in greeting.

His dog wagged its tail, and Jack, a few feet ahead of me, shivered with excitement.

"These must be your tracks I've been cutting since the swamp," the man said cheerfully. "I didn't expect anyone else out here today."

He commented on the frigid temperatures and the effort it took to venture this far into what seemed a pheasant-less plain of squallish, late December.

"Looks like we're the last of the birders," he said. "I owed it to my dog to get out once more."

He chatted amiably about his bird season and inquired about mine. The snow down south along the Snake and Salmon rivers was piling up too, putting a jag in his chukar hunting season.

"It's one of the highest snow years on record," he grinned as he adjusted the flaps on a Stormy Kromer.

His travels, he said, took him through Riggins a week ago where he let his dog loose by the auto yard at the edge of town and the pointer flushed a covey of red legs.

The Stormy Kromer rode on his head like a cushion. He removed a mitten to arrange it, then replaced the leather chopper mitt on his hand.

"We're going to hunt to those trees," he said, gesturing with a vinyl-stock pump gun. "I don't suppose we'll find any birds here today."

I expected to flush one under the lip of the irrigation ditch, I told him.

"So far, not even a track."

We discussed the lay of the land and our place in it, commending ourselves as the last holdouts, then wished each other luck and departed in opposite directions.

A half mile later, and closer to the pickup, Jack angled down the railroad grade and his tail stopped wagging. His rigid body pointed staunchly in a snowy patch of elderberry.

Before I could move toward him, a pheasant jumped noiselessly, flying low under a pillow of wind. I shouldered the gun and swung it over the dog's head. The bird glided across the embankment hugging the railbed before dipping into the swamp.

It all happened very quickly and decisively with one small window for a trigger pull.

I did not shoot.

Instead, I marked where the bird dropped into the marsh, and the dog and I climbed down from the bank of the railbed into the swamp filled with cattails and waist-deep snow. It buried the dog until I broke trail and he followed at my heels. This swamp was a big chunk of submerged land, bent and brown sedges, willow and dogwood. I leaned against the snow and wondered where the bird went. Pushing toward higher ground, I found wing marks and bird tracks under a hawthorn. The dog snorkeled through the snow and I raised my gun, but any bird that was here had moved on. We broke trail toward a high fencerow and then climbed back up to the road where our pickup was parked. Walking on the plowed road surface we took account of where we had been and what we saw: Snow mostly. Distance. An eagle. Another man and his dog. One pheasant. Tracks under a thorny bush.

I would have liked to tell the man about the pheasant in the marsh. Tell him we flushed a bird on this, the last day of the season, but maybe he saw birds too, unexpectedly, and didn't fire his gun.

If he did, the sound was lost in a wind gust.

Jack shook the melted snow from his coat and plopped onto the floorboards with his head resting on the bench seat.

I turned on the heater.

By the time we hit the highway the dog was asleep.

Winter Nights, Whitefish and Raiha

SANDPOINT — Rauno "Ron" Raiha's hands are like saucers.

Thick and knotty, they hang heavily at the end of tree trunk arms and have served Raiha well.

He was a gun maker, machining steel and crafting wooden stocks before he built this home on a ridge overlooking the lake. He did it by himself with a twenty nine dollar Skilsaw, claw hammer and two-dollar level, pouring the concrete foundation one wheelbarrow-load at a time.

He bought the land as a teenager. It was twenty acres of

timber and meadow that rose gradually from Lake Pend Oreille's north shore like a cat arching its back.

The rise was covered in tamarack and alder, pine, fir and poplar. The woods held game and the trees became lumber.

He paid cash for the parcel even though it had no pond — something Raiha would have liked — but he had strong shoulders and those hands, and the combination, he knew, could do anything.

So, he dug a hole in the ground, bent to the task, built contours, lumps and edges, lined it with fabric to catch silt and keep water from seeping out, and when he was through, Rauno watched the rain and snowmelt fill his man-made cirque. He dropped in fish that he netted, introducing small bass, perch and bluegill to their new haunts.

After decades, the pond is still there, and so are the fish. He casts to them when he can't get on the lake that lies below his property blinking through trees and scenting his woods with the aroma of fresh, northern water.

In winter he shovels the snow from the ice on his pond to allow sunlight in. The plants need the light to produce oxygen. Rauno's pond has through the years become a natural system, more or less, he says. He doesn't feed the fish.

"They all eat themselves."

Bugs, minnows and each other.

Rauno is Finnish and before he came to North Idaho he lived near the Baltic Sea where the land, he says, is a lot like the northern reaches of the continental United States. He caught his first pike not far from the place where the Rapala family started its dynasty making top water plugs and the finest filet knives on the planet.

He remembers as a boy using a length of line with a spoon that he shot bolo-like into a lake because he did not own a fishing pole.

"R-r-r-r-r," ... He rolls the R in the back of his throat like a blender... "Rah-pah-lah," he says, to show where the accent lies in the name that many mispronounce, he says. Americans slur the vowels, casually cutting them short.

There is little that is casual about Rauno Raiha, and in the almost fifty years he has lived east of Sandpoint, he has not succumbed to extemporaneous talk or a reliance on serendipity.

Like the Rapala family, whose members were close with his own clan in the old country, Raiha lives life deliberately.

"The first Rapala plug was carved from tree bark with a jackknife," he says.

It lured fish so well that more were carved, meticulously, and handed around to anglers in the region. It's how the enterprise began and eventually became an empire. Today, Rapala fishing gear, lures and knives are one of the few Finnish imports marketed worlwide.

Fishing is part of Finland's heritage, Raiha says. Despite his proclivity for venison and upland game, he prefers fish to any other meat.

As a Finn, he says, eels, eelpout, sheefish and the most undervalued fish in North America, whitefish, are all species he has eaten with relish.

Whitefish especially.

Ask local anglers what they know about Lake Pend Oreille's deep-water whitefish, the most numerous and under-fished species in the lake, and their faces go blank.

Ask them who chases whitefish, and there is just one name that keeps popping up.

"If you want to know about whitefish," someone in town said, "Ron is the guy to talk to."

There are only a few hardy people on the lake who target whitefish, the man said. You can count them on a couple of frozen fingers because whitefish are targeted mostly in winter.

Raiha is number one on the list of North Idaho whitefish anglers.

An autumn trip along the lake to his driveway follows a narrow road that passes red barns and brown livestock. It thins farther along where the forest closes in. Leaves from trembling aspen fall like gold coins in a breeze and hillsides are a vivid orange as if painted with watercolors. The tamarack needles, having dropped from the softwoods, make wet lines on the pavement. Wheels slip and spin as the car climbs a ridge. The sun filters through the canopy like an old movie. Somewhere a violin concerto plays, Sibelius maybe. It fades as the house comes into view.

A large rectangular shed on one side of the driveway is filled with dimensional lumber. Beams and boards are thick and meticulously stacked on stickers.

Wearing bib overalls, Raiha is outside with the chores. A tractor with a Farmi log-pulling winch behind its big wheels shines newly washed.

"Coffee?" he asks, walking out from the gossamer shade of a maple whose leaves make a deeply yellow umbrella.

"I am European," he says, "So the coffee will be strong."

His house is elegant, sharp as a skinning knife, pragmatic and beautiful with Persian rugs and oil paintings from the Baltic region of Russia, Poland, Finland, Sweden and old Germany.

The walls are wood-sided, mitered and stained.

"There is no paint," he says. The fir, cedar and pine of the walls, floor and bookshelves are oiled and stove-heated.

He slips off his Romeo shoes at the door, trading them for house slippers and almost lumbers, with the slow gait of a laborer, through a hall to the kitchen.

Steaming coffee is presented in a porcelain cup on a porcelain saucer. He opens a book of photographs showing a local legend, Bob Selle, whose family homesteaded the valley north of here and who fished whitefish with Raiha for forty years.

"He is gone now," he says as cups quietly clink on saucers.

The coffee steams in shafts of mottled light from the windows.

Raiha has taken his fascination with whitefish to great lengths. He has dived to the lake's bottom where he has watched lake whitefish roll on their sides pushing stones out of the way with their possum like snouts to better snatch squiggling, mud-bottom insect larvae with tiny mouths.

He has studied the lake's whitefish for decades and has enough material for a book that would educate fishery biologists, he says, but he has lost interest in writing it. Billed as inconsequential except among historical-fish purists, the lake's whitefish don't exude sex appeal or draw dollars.

They instead are homely, almost bookish, spending days in the quiet halls of the underwater world where fancy lures, spendy boats and well-paid guides can't entice them. Whitefish aren't included on social media videos and if you ask most anglers, they don't know the fish exists, or they don't care to know. The many pictures and mounts of the lake's bounty that hang in local taverns, restaurants, barber and bait shops don't include whitefish. The trophy mounts are mostly big rainbows, sometimes passels of kokanee, pike and bass. Every now and then they include as eye candy a picture of a large mackinaw, a species targeted for removal by the state's fishery department.

Lake whitefish may comprise the bulk of fish in Lake Pend Oreille, but despite being related to salmon, whitefish are considered a rough fish, an unwanted species that spends most of the year spread over great depths where anglers don't go.

During the winter and early spring, lake whitefish gather in shallows to spawn on gravel beds, but most of the year they are a challenge to catch.

Raiha knows this and more.

The Lake Superior whitefish was introduced to Pend Oreille in 1898 in an effort to start a commercial fishery, Raiha says.

The fishery took off for a while, but interest fell flat after a freak flood sent kokanee into Pend Oreille, flushed down from Flathead Lake in Montana. Kokanee — a sweet-fleshed landlocked salmon that grows to fourteen inches or more — became the new rage.

Before that, however, loggers, out of work in the winter, found another occupation to keep them busy. Along with the region's unemployed workers they swarmed the frozen lake chasing whitefish for cash. They towed shanties and sleds from shore, stayed on the ice in tents and fished through chopped holes. Their catch was loaded into twenty-pound boxes that filled boxcars of trains heading east, thousands of pounds at a time, Raiha says.

The Evans Brothers — not the coffee makers — had a smokehouse where the fish were cured for the trip, and for local consumption.

The fishery was so popular for a time that the state's only whitefish hatchery was located on Lake Pend Oreille. But those stories are tarnished with age, Raiha says, they are like voices echoing from shore. They are the sound of a splitting maul in a block of birch that creeps across the glassine water as you sit in a kayak on the hushed lake in winter spooling a hand line. The ka-wack floats over otherwise silent beaches piled with wave ice. It is a fragile, lonely sound as cold as the black water that motionless buoys your hull.

Like much history, and to some extent the fish itself, Raiha says, the story of the lake's whitefish is not wanted and no longer learned.

People on wave runners and forty-foot sloops, Chris Crafts and ski-boats prefer tales of Gerrard rainbows from spicy sport anglers. They want glitz and jumping fish that strip line from screaming reels as sports respond with wild whooping. Sun peels the skin on their backs as they pump bottle beers from big, ice-filled coolers taking pictures with cell phones on a lake better known now for real estate than resolution.

As a county marine deputy who oversees twenty officers, Raiha spends his summer on the water saving tourists from themselves.

In winter he is on the lake alone, his aluminum skiff anchored at both ends as he hovers in the dark over eighty feet of icy black liquid reeling in whitefish by hand.

He catches enough fish in the three to eight-pound range – the six-plus pound state record was caught in Lake Pend Oreille, but records don't interest Raiha – to keep and eat.

"They are tricky to catch, so it's a challenge to get them," he says.

He eats the mild-tasting flesh whenever the chance arises.

"I am a Finlander," he says, "I eat fish soup, fried fish, smoked fish, baked fish, any way you can imagine. I smoke them hard as jerky, or soft so you can eat them as a meal at the dinner table."

Many anglers who incidentally snag whitefish as they chase money species like Gerrard rainbows, kill and dump them on shore for the birds to eat.

"I would rather throw the trout on the shore," Raiha says. "I value whitefish more."

Winter mornings he shoves off around midnight when the sky is a swirl of stars and his breath is thin smoke that makes crystals on warm skin. Before the first exhaust stack flutters on a log truck in a trailer court at the edge of town, before coffee gurgles in a pot at the diner, or the newspaper carriers throw the morning edition on a sidewalk, he has cut a wake to his whitefish haunts, and he is bobbing out there somewhere in the shell of a boat like a castaway.

He returns when schoolchildren slide sleepily from warm beds. When school bus lights blink on the road below his house he is home cleaning fish.

If the shore is a juggernaut of frozen spray, he drags a thirty five-pound kayak to the beach sliding it onto the ice-fringed water that a boat on a trailer cannot access. Using a compass to navigate in a starless night more than a mile to his fishing grounds, he heads across a lake that seems viscous as cooking oil.

Raiha had a charter fishing business on the Kenai Peninsula once. He worked as a ski instructor, too, and moved to Idaho for an opportunity to learn how to make guns. He built his home, raised a family. His daughter is a civil engineer in Alaska and fishes in her spare time.

"The apple didn't fall far from the tree," he says.

The reason whitefish remain numerous in the lake and are rarely caught, with a state record hovering under seven pounds, is simple, Raiha says.

"No one knows how to fish for them," he says. "You have to go out at night."

In the winter, fishers must use a hand line because whitefish bites barely register.

"You can't fish with gloves on," he says.

Hands ache from the cold and from the sharp spears of fraggle ice that form on the line. If a boat heater is brought along, anglers must be careful to keep the fishing line away from the heater, Raiha cautions. When a whitefish is hooked, line is spooled onto the angler's lap in a neat circle that freezes together. The fish is unhooked and flipping and flopping, is stowed, while the weighted hook is re-baited with wool and a maggot before it is once again, carefully, dropped overboard. The line unspools into the lake's maw, slipping through ungloved hands, peeling slushy splinters, it snakes to depths of eighty or a hundred feet. On these shoals whitefish gather at night to eat larvae. Hours later, escaping the morning light, they return to water three hundred feet below the surface.

"Whitefish have very photosensitive eyes," Raiha says.

And their meat is firm and extremely palatable.

"So delicate," he says.

He caught a thirty-pound sheefish – named 'unknown fish' by early explorers sheefish are the largest members of the whitefish subfamily – fifty miles above the Arctic Circle a few years back.

"The biggest whitefish I ever caught," he says. "We ate whitefish for weeks. It was fantastic."

On this lake though, he is after the smaller ones, a few at a time so they don't spoil because the flesh of these fish does not store well, even when it's frozen, Raiha says. It quickly loses its texture and firmness.

Alone in a boat in the dark miles from his launch with gloveless hands feeling for a bite under a sky that dazzles stars or is as black as the water lapping quietly against his hull, Raiha anticipates the tug he knows will come.

"You almost have to get your mind down there with them," he says.

After gently tugging back, setting the hook into the whitefish's fleshy snorkel-like mouth, Raiha hand over hand pulls in the fishing line, coiling it in his lap.

It stiffens and freezes in the winter air as Raiha quietly brings his quarry, wriggling, to the side of the boat.

TANK CREEK

Beer and Ice Fishing

You just want to drink beer and ice fish.

It's been on your mind since the temperatures dropped like a splitting maul and snowflakes wisped sparsely through the concrete-cold days. You've considered loading the five-gallon buckets, the ones used for lard in a commercial bakery, or the blue ones that contained wheel grease or ninety-weight transmission oil. Load them with ice-fishing poles, smelly bait putty, a down vest, extra winter socks and a can of maggots.

The buckets have the tops removed and were cleaned out with the high-pressure hose at the car wash years ago.

One of the buckets, crammed under a lawn chair in the yard shed, is full of rusty nails from a summer project. Another is in the enclosed porch stuffed with stocking caps and woolen mittens.

Tip their contents into a pile on the floor and load them with fishing line, Swedish pimple jigs, lead heads with rubber bodies, bobbers — the tiny ones — and sinkers.

You may have to snorkel through the dim light of the garage in your stocking feet, uncomfortably shuffling on the sticky cement floor while cold bites toes and fingers, to find the tote that says fishing gear. Root through it with a flashlight in your mouth for monofilament, a plastic box of jigs with silver blades and a bottle of garlic juice to entice finicky spiny rays.

Place these gently into the bed of the same pickup truck you owned when you fished the grimy five-gallon buckets out of the dumpsters behind Snively's bakery and the truck shop.

The pickup is parked on the slab in the driveway banked with snow. It's an older model Ford with side panels made to look like real wood. The upholstery is ragged, covered with a Western-style seat cover that imitates a horse blanket. It sports a faux leather divider and pouches near the floorboards that hide an array of gear.

If you need a screwdriver look there.

Or pliers.

You may find a brand new spool of twelve-pound test fluorocarbon in one of those seat-cover pockets, several unopened packets of fly line leaders and tippets, shotgun shells for twelve and twenty gauge guns and a handful of purple, sixteen-gauge shells for a break-open single shot you no longer own. You'll find Q-tips, melted chapstick, a roll of black electrician's tape, lottery tickets with unreadable barcodes, assorted bullets for several calibers including a half-full box of rimfires from the time you took the kids plinking. They were in middle school. Here's the target folded into a small square with holes peppered around the likeness of a gopher. A pocket knife, "Man, I've been looking for this forever." Bottle caps, an Aerosmith cassette tape and others you forgot you had.

Here are sinkers, too. Lots of them. And swivels. "Where were these when I needed them?" A broken plastic cover for the ice auger blade. Grocery store receipts back to ... "Geezus, I remember that day." ... There's a fingernail clipper, a cracked pocket mirror and lint-covered dog biscuits. Jammed into a corner with a bottle of fruit-flavored indigestion tablets is a P-38 can opener, pocket change welded with melted chocolate from a protein bar, a handful of spey flies in a sandwich bag, and a wedding ring.

Huh?

"So, that's where that went."

You hold it for a while, feel its weight and dissect the years you've gone without it as creeping clouds in the sky, a sheet of cirrostratus, edge across the sun.

But you just want to ice fish and drink beer.

The ice auger you've had since high school is in the rafters of the yard shed. You leave post holes in the calf-deep snow from the garage to the shed's wide door that is frozen to the jambs. You jiggle, then put your shoulder against it.

Inside, stepping on a pile of patio cushions covering the stacked steel chairs you finagle the blue auger with the red handle from a bunch of two-by-fours you've stored in the rafters along with staves for the garden tomatoes, a banister you saved from a set of stairs, and one cross-country ski pole.

"C'mon baby. Easy now."

How in the heck did you get it up here?

You move one foot onto the engine of the garden tiller as you climb higher, then yank and jiggle until the swirly steel auger gives, knocking down the staves, spilling a hem-fir stud and the clay pigeon thrower that now hangs by one of its three shiny legs.

The ice auger's two cutting blades are rusted. You haven't used it in a while. Grab the bucket, dump out the nails and head to the truck.

There's a hitch in January called a fishing license.

The license from a week ago won't work.

This realization strikes after you filled up with gas, placed a six-pack of eighteen-ounce brews into the buckets alongside the auger and now you're on your way out of town whistling a song you don't know the words to when you realize the fishing license in your billfold has expired.

The reality of your potential lawlessness strikes you like a bad cast with a bucktail jig. It leaves a bruise but won't draw blood. Not yet.

The sunny sky earlier in the day is now aluminum siding with fatter clouds turning gray. The clear morning that warmed the pavement has become a muddle of squirrel fur.

Is that a snowflake?

Your destination is a half-hour away.

Turning back to find a place that sells a fishing license will take an hour, and you don't want trouble.

Pulling the pickup into a church parking lot near the on-ramp of the highway you consider options.

All you want is to ice fish and drink beer.

If you had your cell phone, you could purchase the license online but – along with an extra pair of leather-insulated Wells Lamont mittens and a spare stocking cap – you left the phone, an artifact of technology and intrusion, on the kitchen counter.

Good riddance.

It is the weekend, business calls will go unanswered. There's no cell phone reception anyhow. Not on a lake bowled in by mountains.

You could go back the way you came, smile, wait at the red lights and the stop signs, wave at discourteous drivers who take a left turn to your right of way, follow the speed limit as a pickup truck with big, Disneyland wheels rides your bumper like it's the drive-through at Jack-in-the Box.

Instead of heading back to the subdivision, you could take the roundabout to the bait shop, but you'll have to mosey into the parking lot, find a spot and stand in line at the license counter behind the bearded honchos from out of state pretending they have lived here long enough to pay the local rate.

"Can you check the number once more?"

"I moved here when Jerry Brown was governor."

You'll have to do it again going the other way.

Weekends are not made for momentous decisions like this one. Leave those to midweek. On Fridays, accords can be salted with the recognition that a two-day weekend is the parachute that softens any pending arbitration.

Saturdays and Sundays are made for introspection, for healing and holy rolling, for walking on water.

Idling in the church parking lot as feathers of snow now zigzag from the sky, this realization is the acknowledgment you need. It recalls prophets, fishers of men and a sprinkling of the divine. Hard water and ichthys, or pisces, depending on your bent and preferred apostle.

It speaks of potluck casseroles in a church basement, the aroma of canned coffee and a soft dependence on pastry hour. Canticles, winter sports on TV and ice fishing.

In the warm cab of a pickup truck loaded with buckets, all the trappings for a few hours on a lake, you reach a consensus based on everything you know about charity.

You vow to be beholden.

Maybe in the future – no big decisions today – you will offer yourself up as a church usher, wrapped in the promise of forgiveness.

That settles it.

Thank you, Lord.

You check the bed of the pickup one last time for anything that may tip, roll or take flight, but mostly to take account, and to whiff the still humid air in a day that has become leaden. Crawling back into the cab, you click a seat belt, move the shifter on the steering column and trounce on the gas pedal as the truck wobbles toward the four-lane.

The lake ice at your destination, you're certain, is clear with just a skiff of snow and it's hard as a railroad spike. It waits for your footfalls and outlawry. It waits for the crunching sounds of boots, the swish-swish of the auger cutting a hole, and the comfort of a bucket seat.

You anticipate dropping a small green jig, tipped with a maggot, into the chasm of black water and letting the bobber make tiny rings as you jiggle it.

The silence of the cold and the quiet of the pine-fringed lake are compass points.

Along with a couple of beers, they are all you need right now.

Blood In The Tracks

The slick was as big as a tractor tire. A deep slush red frozen into the hardpack snow. It wasn't there the night before when I climbed the steep incline that Raleigh Hughes once in 1952 rumbled up while sitting in the steel seat of a bulldozer.

But the next morning when I drove down the mountain it stained the road like automatic transmission fluid.

I stepped from the pickup to examine the icy, blood-stained blot as if a deer had bled out, it being January and at least a month since the close of hunting season.

It reminded me of Raleigh's story. Of how, more than fifty years earlier, before hydraulics made operating machinery easier, Raleigh was on his way home after an overnight snow. He had gotten his car stuck on this same mountain road, which, back then, remained unplowed most of the winter.

He decided to walk the five miles to his ranch when he happened upon a bulldozer.

This occurred in the years following the Big One in which Raleigh served on a naval observation boat in the South Pacific. After the war he returned to St. Maries, married, had children and managed a mountain ranch where he raised his family and livestock. Raleigh had no occasion to operate a crawler tractor, the kind that clanked and belched and used a friction system to control the steel-padded tracks. All he knew when he came upon the snowbound machine was that he was immobile despite the chains on the tires of his car, and that he must get back to the ranch where his wife, Ardys, and the couple's children lived.

But the road was blown out with snow piled higher the farther up in elevation he climbed. The walking was harsh, drifts filled his pockets, moisture seeped through his pants and his shoes were sopping wet.

The car had mired on the lip of an incline just above a creek that boiled and bubbled through a culvert as it made its way to the river. It was the same creek that miles upstream ran behind his barn.

Jumping from the sideboard of the car, Raleigh decided to navigate the drifted road that wound along the canyon and gained ground before flattening out. From the top of the plateau he could follow the swales east to his ranch.

He had not walked a half mile, the deep furrows of his movement behind him, when he came upon the bulldozer and Raleigh got a notion.

He climbed aboard and, always mechanically inclined, found the primer and throttle. When he heeled the starter switch the engine fired sooty smoke in belches as if from a coal bin and the big diesel roared.

He brushed snow from the steel seat, let loose on the throttle, dropped the great iron blade and away he went.

At 83, he laughs about it. He embraced this unexpected good fortune.

During the two years that Raleigh spent in the South Pacific waiting to get blown by a Japanese torpedo into the shark blue ocean so dangerously placid and warm, Ardys, the woman he loved, waited in Idaho sending her thoughts like electricity in Raleigh's direction. Through devil cold and summer's heat, the couple never lost hope of being reunited.

So, here he was now, Pacific salt washed from his shirt collar, sitting with wet pants and shoes on top of a frigid and purloined hunk of industry, belching exhaust on his way through a backwoods landscape to see her. She was his wife now, had bore his children and was probably, he surmised, scrubbing diapers in Hells Gulch Creek that twisted back through a grove of poplars behind the corral.

The snow got deep that winter and he didn't get to town often to buy the Copenhagen he still keeps tucked between his lip and gum.

"Everything will kill you," he says with a smile. "This is the least of it."

His wife sent him down the mountain to St. Maries a day earlier to purchase goods for the cupboard — flour, baking soda, sugar. Tobacco being prominent on the list. Brandy if there was money to spare.

Raleigh had traveled the ten miles to collect the provender. He had stayed overnight to avoid the pending storm and, with the threat over, was pushing his way that morning through new snow, the caterpillar tractor roaring, clearing a path, belching a string of black exhaust over the top of his head as he returned to his doorstep.

The experience was enlivening.

Eventually, he sat on the seat of his own bulldozer and in a flat, well-watered plain across the road from his farmyard, he flattened an expanse of tamarack, knocking down the trees, pulling the rootballs and planting hay grass in the newly-tilled field below Grassy Mountain.

It is on this swath of meadow that I live.

The field he cut along a ridge of tamarack and pine, tangled with crab apples and wild roses has my house now and barn, wood shed and corral.

Back then, a half century ago, Raleigh felled all the pecker pole larch that covered the fifteen-acre meadow like dog hair. Setting the slash on fire, he dumped offal — cow guts and slipped hides from butchering — to lure bear and coyotes that he shot with a rifle from his porch across the dirt road.

He resides in town now, and often stops me to ask, "How's the ranch?"

It seems like a lifetime ago since he homed there, his children have made their own children, and moved away.

I don't tell him of the blood slick on the road.

People got to eat, he'd say through a sly grin, certainly speaking from experience.

In winter, back when Raleigh kept the ranch, elk came down from the mountain and gathered on the bench where he farmed. They roamed the creek edges and found the hay he piled in stacks. Timothy and fescue ripened during summer in the adjacent, once-forested fields he and his brothers cleared with a dozer later on. The men's effort turned acres of timberland into crops that Raleigh sold, or used to feed his cattle through the winter.

These elk, though, relatively new to the region — earlier herds, never abundant, were shot or pushed out — preferred his hay to the browse in the hills.

The chestnut-maned ungulates, big deer brought in by boxcar and released in the mountains of North Idaho were, at least to ranchers like Raleigh, less commodity than nuisance. They bored into haystacks destroying feed, they busted fences, and spooked cows.

Strict elk harvesting seasons had been established to burgeon the new herds and to keep hunters in check. The state accorded the animals as highly valuable and punitive measures prevented people like Raleigh from contravening.

Instead, he regularly complained to local game officials, and with dour persistance the wildlife officer assigned to Raleigh's neck of the woods emphasized the animals belonged to the government whose regulations must be honored.

One day, the warden returned to follow up on a grievance and silently viewed the damage to Raleigh's fences and his winter store of hay.

The man stood in the snow wearing his lace-up boots, curt

Western hat and a short woolen coat. He knocked burned tobacco from his pipe.

"As a government agent, my hands are tied," he said for the umpteenth time, but there was a spark in his demeanor as he packed the bowl of his pipe with fresh tobacco.

The warden turned to Raleigh and lowered his voice as if out of habit or prudence.

"I am equally want to take action," he whispered, "if you up and develop a taste for elk meat."

After lighting his pipe the warden climbed into his Army surplus truck and drove away.

Raleigh and his family accepted the man's offer and his discretion, knocking down the occasional bull, spilling blood in the snow, enjoying elk steaks for a few years before the state opened a general elk-hunting season. The hunt provided Raleigh with an opportunity to collect thirty five dollars a day carrying dudes on horseback into the hills. That was real money then, he said.

Canvas tents and axes, oil lanterns and bed rolls, cast iron skillets and pots for stew and spud chowder. The city hunters paid Raleigh for his skill to prop a stout meat pole, skin and quarter.

"Those hunters had it pretty good," he said. "And things started looking up for us as well."

The episode of frozen blood in the road was relayed over coffee in the county commissioner's office.

Sitting in the wooden chairs, one floor below the only courtroom and judge's chambers, a small audience during a gab session was told of the blood and of the urgent, copper-colored boot tracks that stamped it with fear and adrenaline.

The hilljack who tossed the empty shell casing must have heard the gunshot echo like a landslide down the valley to the new homes glowing in the moonless night. Working quickly with a folding knife while slipping on the blood that pooled in the bed of the pickup, he loaded the carcass and sped away.

"Damned poacher," someone said.

"Desperate and out for meat," offered an administrator seated in a hard chair on a floor that creaked.

Normally, in other years, the game department may have been summoned, but given this fiasco of what the newspapers call an economy, acquaintance with despair has become a vital slice of the bottom line.

"At some point, everyone needs a leg up," a county commissioner added with untranscribed elegance. It requires a bit of wisdom on the part of the rule makers, he said, while pointing at the ceiling.

With equal horse sense, Raleigh, a half century earlier, hoisted himself into the iron seat of the crawler tractor whose ownership wasn't questioned or considered. Instead, he punched the throttle and climbed the many miles to his wife and kids.

The acuity of the game warden resulted in the set of elk antlers, bone white now, on the prow of his barn. It added campfire sparks to the starfall of autumn nights in elk camp. It made years nominal without the weight of misfortune.

"Somewhere back in each of our histories, we can attest to blood in our tracks," a commissioner said.

The judge, who had come down from upstairs and seated himself in one of the the hard chairs, didn't blush at the words.

He agreed.

Scab Mountain Chukar

We hunt Scab Mountain, the usual place, where a two track climbs to the sky through short grass along the edge of a cliff.

The birdseye view of the canyon outside the passenger door makes turning around seem the most pragmatic of options. Heading back downhill would prevent neck hairs from vibrating like a Jimi Hendricks guitar solo, a fear only blacktop can assuage.

We have learned to keep going despite the additional dread of meeting a pickup truck head-on. Because the hillside rises abruptly on one side and drops astonishingly on the other, there is no room on the narrow two-track for a turnout. Just sky, and somewhere far below is a river. A nose-to-nose encounter with another pickup, even a small economy job, would result in a stand-off. To relieve the two-vehicle gridlock, a rig could either back uphill for a half mile or more, or the one pointed uphill could back a half-mile or more down.

Such impasses allow the drivers of both vehicles to revisit

transcendental questions as cloud shadows slide across their hoods like knives on a whetstone.

Would a second Jimmy Carter term have edged Billy Beer into the domestic brew market? Can bacon bring our nation together?

Lonesome theology seasoned with hillbilly epistemology is credited for the many antique farm implements rusting in fields along our nation's highways.

Today, however, the last day of January and the final day of the Idaho chukar season, we are blessed with a dearth of snow, an unobstructed road and a determination to thoughtlessly grind on.

We are after gamebirds that, if they had the capacity, would laugh at us, point primary feathers and weep like jackals from their basalt perches at the first sign of our apprehension.

They are demons, these chukar birds that live on the windblown edge of the universe. "Chukah!" they yell. "Ka-chuk ka-chuk," like a horse running through rocky hills on steel shoes, or a two-cycle engine sputtering in an effort to fire.

"Chuk chuk chuk chuk aw."

We allow them no such gratification. Instead we grasp the steering wheel like a rabbit's foot, exhale in a soft sweeping whisper, press our feet against the floorboards and limply wend toward a postage stamp parking spot in a scrub meadow we know is there.

It is almost noon when we reach the place with enough elbow room finally to wheel around.

Another pickup, its cab empty, a vacuous blue reflected in

its windshield, has beaten us to the place.

"Early risers," we grouse.

The old Ford is obviously the rig of a savvy bird-getter who arrived efficiently and probably alone without hours of highway behind him. Likely a local hunter with a well-mannered spaniel sitting quietly in the front seat, as opposed to the yipping psychopath of the pointing variety shivering with anticipation in a kennel in our pickup's bed, and a sleeping boy with a cheek glued to the window.

Wearing old boots, shirts spotted with coffee stains and orange vests sporting broken zippers, our pockets bulge with a mish mash of shotshells we collected back home. The shells appeared randomly, like mold, in glove boxes and coffee cans, in garage cupboards, under car seats and in kitchen drawers far from the well-meaning ammo rack on the gun case where they belonged. We stuffed them into our pockets.

Our disheveled presentation indicates killing fowl is our priority, not a photoshoot in a glamor magazine.

When we open the pickup truck doors, most of our gear tumbles into the dirt, heralding our arrival.

The clean Snake River wind which greets us on these occasions is a salient mixture of distance and history. It barrels up the canyon showering us with the sweet aroma of grasses and dry ground, hard scrabble stuff that hints of longing and adventure. It reminds us that, as the day drags on, we will be rendered like bear fat. By evening, our face and hands will be wind slicked with a coating of dry chafe. Our eyelids will swell with dirt, dust and grass slivers that are

the ingredients of a hearty, wind-borne stew. After hours
of hunting on these gusty inclines we will glisten red as the
snubbed hood of an Econoline.

When the boy awakes, we place a twelve-gauge pump action
in his hands, slam a shell into the chamber, check the safety
and point him to a skinny trail that flanks the shorn, grassy
mountainside like a blood vein.

Follow that, we say, we're right behind you.

We are not, of course, right behind him.

Mortals of a certain age must navigate terrain that a
teenager floats over. The boy quickly becomes an orange-
vested speck in the distance, a place from which we hear the
occasional bang through flagging gusts as we trip, slip and
curse trying to keep up.

Chukar inhabit steep, unsteady ground with lots of loose
rocks teetering on the angle of repose, slippery and clumpish
grasses, jags and trip ups that hunters don't notice while
scaling hillsides. They are watching for nuances in a pointing
dog that may indicate birds ahead. Footing, however, is
paramount, and inattention makes for sketchy going.

I remind myself of this as I lay on my back on a small
basalt-sharded knoll, eyes skyward after averting a downhill
somersault. Luckily I have taken a spill on a relatively flat
piece of real estate on a hillside that is otherwise steep as
the back of a coffee maker. A thousand feet below me is the
moving puddle; an iconic river heralded for the canyons it has
cut in its quest for the sea. From this position, the result of
a slip on crumble rock, I uncomfortably examine the gouge

in my otherwise deeply lacquered shotgun stock. A sharp stone, like the ones pressing through my flannel shirt, left a dime size dent in the walnut, but there is no time to grieve the cheerlessness of this finding.

I roust myself, pick rock chips from my elbow and give chase to the birds I know exist somewhere in this talus-strewn land. The dog for the time being sets aside any hard feelings caused by being kennelled in the back of the pickup for hours. He transforms into a sleek silent rocket scrambling up and down the mountain in front of me.

When he stops on a dime beside a pile of gray stone, I encourage his generous mood.

"Hold it there buddy. I'm on my way," I say with one hand on the pistol grip of my gun as the other is an awkward ballast to steady myself on a scratched-out trail heading in the dog's direction.

Squeezed between the razor sharp point of the German shorthair, and my reluctant footfalls, the birds see an opening, break and run while the dog, in stop and start spurts, attempts to corner them. They flush and tumble downhill like grapeshot.

Considering it my duty to at least play along in what more and more seems a futile game, I point and pull the trigger of the over and under gun and am knocked on my butt as I slip on the hardscrabble slope.

The birds keep going with the dog following over a cliff and into oblivion.

The boy is above me somewhere on the main trail, a well-used and sturdy route that avoids the barren steepness I cling to. He follows its easy-going, grassy lip around the side of the mountain.

The birds up there are well versed in the hunting sport, at least today. His is likely the same trail trod by the hunter whose Ford is parked next to our pickup truck.

Occasionally I hear shots and a moan of dejection from above followed by the whistling sound of wind being spilled through coverts as birds, invisible before cresting the plateau, careen past hugging contours like tiny fighter jets.

I attempt to turn as a flock clocks by at thirty knots. With a downhill boot on unsturdy ground, I take a shot and tumble briefly while protecting the walnut stock from more rock bites.

This kind of jovial, full-contact hunting really gets your blood boiling. Rising from the dirt like a punch drunk fighter I unsteadily move toward the fury that is my shorthair pointer.

In a small tangled fold where a rivulet bursts from the side of the hill, the dog kicks up a quail which I dispatch quickly because I fear falling, and the lack of thinking does wonders for my shot.

The pointer brings back the quarry but, deciding to take a water break, drops the bird into a mudhole. The bird's usually-gay plumage turns several shades of wet and ugly.

When we return hours later to our truck parked in the lonely spot of grass at the lip of the canyon, the other pickup is gone. The boy is grumpy as he drops his vest into our truck's bed and unloads his gun. His hike along the trail has been long with nothing to show for it except the sweaty ring on his ball cap, the blisters on his feet and a weariness in his shotgun arm.

It's apparent he can use a triple deluxe burger from the joint in Lewiston where we usually stop on the way home.

As we wait for our hunting partner to return to the rig, I pull the muddy quail from my vest and set it on the tailgate. It is a pathetic little bird that will nonetheless make a fine vittle.

"Hunting is a bit like life, you gotta get off the easy trail if you want to see success," I evangelize as if the thought is divinely inspired. "You know what I'm saying?"

My bruised elbow and chipped gun stock are worth another piece of pedagoguery.

"Collect a few dings. Take some hits," I sigh.

The boy examines my dented gun stock, flaked lacquer and torn shirt sleeve. He eyes the forlorn little quail on the tailgate.

"That's not a real good example of success, Dad," he says.

It is barely a crumb on the corner of the mouth of accomplishment, I silently acknowledge.

"But it's better than a poke in the eye with a sharp stick," I counter, rubbing a scratch on my eyelid.

There were a lot of birds and many shots. We worked the dog and crawled across some beautiful country that a lot of people never see. I remind him of this and watch as he sternly considers these musings.

"Are we going to stop at the burger place?" he replies.

Break Up

Al's Toms

It's just Al now.

His boys are grown, making their own families.

But there was a time when spring found Al in the woods with a son sitting between his knees on the damp ground. A few yards away, at the edge of an alley of firs, another son sat with his back against bark and a shotgun tottering on his knees.

There might have been a shhh on Al's lips and then a scratch on a slate call, and maybe a cut and yelp from the reed in his mouth as a cloud shadow crossed the bridge of his nose.

There was a bunch of those boys. Four sons, maybe five, that Al brought into the woods one at a time, on occasion more, to learn to talk turkey.

When Al moved into the country from out East, almost a half century ago, he was known for diphthongs stacked up like traffic when he pronounced "Boston" or "coffee." His consonants became vowels in "car" or "butter,"

He traveled to Idaho for a teaching degree at the state's

flagship university in Moscow and the first time he heard of an opportunity to gun for toms, he rode his memory back to the outdoor magazines he paged as a child.

Names like Osceola, Gould's and Rio Grande were recalled along with the dim light of a bulb on a bed stand, the musty smell of an attic room where siblings snored as he turned pages of the Field & Stream magazine he kept under his mattress.

For that first turkey hunt an old pickup took him to the bumpy land south and east of Lewiston on a high plateau rimmed with pines. It introduced him to a brand of bird called Merriam's on the Joseph Plains, a wide palm of knuckle-short grass with breaks of deep slants and crevasses that fall into the Snake River on one side and the Salmon on another.

He didn't kill a tom.

"It was sort of a buck fever," he explains.

But he learned he could speak the language.

He was one of the early hunters to pick up turkey talk and it hinged him like a door to that place, which was at the time one of few areas in Idaho with a legal turkey hunting season.

He took up residence on those slopes along the edges — always the edges — of the yellow pine and greening sunflowers, Douglas clover, larkspur and boletus, chanterelles and syringa.

He learned nuances along the way: How hens dallied on their rendezvous with a gobbling tom, yelping as they came, picking lethargic bugs from the dew wet grass, snapping at pine seeds, turkey necks like swivel sticks, their eyes like magnets attracted to movement.

A tom might meet them halfway.

Luring the tom close enough for Al's shotshell was magic. Sometimes he lured a hen first, and she dragged a tom to gun range.

It was Al sitting with his back against a tree as morning shadows edged a feeding lane, green paint on his face, the shotgun perilous and ancient, its mechanism smooth, its wooden stock slick to the grip.

Using a mouth reed, box call or by rubbing a stick on slate to imitate the wanna-call of a hen, Al coaxed a tom closer.

It's better over here, he would say with the reed and the slate. "C'mon over."

Or, "See for yourself, see for yourself."

The long beard, always one of those, would turn blue in the face, would wag and fan. The bird's booming was a bass speaker in Al's chest.

It's been many years since Al's first time on the Plains, and a handful of years since the last time he visited that place in the spring, he says.

The learning he handed down long ago.

Al has a hankering to drive his old pickup down there again, bumping the two track through mist and starlight. Maybe alone this time like it was in the beginning, at the edge of the greening forest leaving tracks in the frost, snow patches or early dew as morning's umber light sifts through limbs of pine, falls into the Selway Bitterroot, casts shadows in the Gospel

Hump and Frank Church, and tumbles across the Joseph Plains like a countenance. Maybe snow. Maybe rain. Who knows? Does it matter?

He has a few grandkids, he says.

It might be time to sit them quietly between Papa's knees as a hen decoy bobs in a breeze where the grass mixes with pine and fir cones and the slate call says peep peep. The reed call in Al's mouth cackles like a bird coming off a roost, followed by soft yelps.

When a gobbler slips in, the child's eyes grow big.

"I was still, just like Papa said."

And Al is all mouth call, softly purring, until the tom's face flushes amethyst and its waddle blushes like raspberry sorbet. It fans a tail and drags a foot like a receiver.

The wind from the canyon blows strands of the bird's lichen-like beard.

Al, his cheek on the smooth wooden stock, an eye squinting, whispers.

"Cover your ears."

Morning In The Garage

The neighbor's pickup revs once and before you open your eyes it passes your driveway, heading out of town.

You hear a songbird, probably awakened by the truck, flute a single note and likely fluff itself for a few more minutes of shut-eye.

It's not yet five in the morning and this can only mean one thing.

Your neighbor, a man who takes advantage of every hunting season to lockstep into the forest a time or two, to maybe raise a stand, peer through a scope or binoculars, chamber shells into the rifles or shotguns he carries before returning home with fresh-air glow on his cheeks, is off to the turkey woods.

This weekend he heads to a small chunk of land of which he is the sole proprietor. It is a honey hole, a sweet spot with gumdrops hanging from the limbs of trees and the gurgle of a sweet soda fountain. It is the homing ground of a flock of tom turkeys with ten-inch beards and marvelous fanned tails that, mounted and displayed just right, would cover a wall in a man cave once the family pictures and oil paintings from community college art classes are boxed and moved to the garage. The cave may be spacious enough for antlers and a stuffed crappie, maybe a kit fox hide hanging by the door, a coonskin cap on a hook by the plasma TV. It's a work in progress and reason enough to keep the shotgun and the decoy bag, the camo vest with the padded seat and pocketful of turkey calls on duty in the back of the extended cab pickup truck.

When the notion strikes, all that's required for a quick jaunt to the forest is to rub sleep from puffy eyes, adjust the camo clothing you slept in, jump into a pair of boots, turn the ignition key and press the accelerator before neighborhood coffee pots hiss and gurgle.

The roar of your neighbor's pickup escaping swiftly and secretively into the fog through the light of streetlamps has you standing in the dark bedroom wondering.

What if you followed suit and quickly threw your kit together, could you still make it to the river knoll before first light where you killed the tom turkey last year? Or maybe to the flat above the lake where the swaggering jake surprised the boy and you as it danced like a gigolo in a disco bar before dashing whippet-like into the syringa without a single gun raised. Better yet, could you appear before the sun at the forested saddle above the logging road where a raft of birds lives annually undisturbed?

You're in your underwear in the hallway but not for long. You sneak back into the bedroom, open dresser drawers while peeling off a t-shirt and replacing it with a camo long-sleeved thermal. At the same time bouncing on one foot, you pull on a pair of Helly Hansen ultra hot long johns that keep you warm even in a cold spring rain. Your anticipation almost trips you at the stairs that you hobble down in the dark, waking the dog from a whimpering dream on his cushion where he purports to guard the place.

You intuitively reach for the garage doorknob in the dark, find it, then stand barefoot on cold concrete. You hit the light switch and learn the bulb isn't bright enough to illuminate the turkey gear you stowed a year ago in the nooks of shelves, on coat hooks and between big plastic totes.

These eleventh-hour forays are instructive. They reinforce the attractive qualities you attributed to your spouse long ago, namely her power of observation.

Alone in the garage, though, two flights of stairs from the warmth of the comforter, you find a moment to reevaluate.

Just because your office desk collects an assortment of bric-a-brac like newspapers, magazines, random letters and receipts, rifle cartridges, greenish bones collected from forest adventures, piles of pens and stained coffee cups, none of it has any bearing on the organization you employ when it comes to your most cherished pastime.

This you tell yourself.

Right now, on a stack of courthouse Bibles, you will devoutly swear that your hunting and fishing gear is warehoused, sharp as a tack. It is ironed, pleated, and filed to such a degree of precision that account executives nod their approval.

No snelled hook, arrow fletching, BB or boot lace is unaccounted for.

"Ask me," you tell your wife. "Ask me where my stuff is."

"Sure," she says. "Where is your stuff?"

"I know exactly where," you reply.

But you don't.

It is frighteningly apparent, as you stand barefoot on the cold concrete in the faint light, that you have lost the striker for your slate call. Your entire collection of mouth reeds is gone and, poof, your turkey decoys, too, have seemingly sneaked into the cinderblock. Where are they? What about your face paint and the flossy veil that keeps bugs from tickling your nostrils and the sun off your face?

And where are your camo cargo pants?

They were hanging here yesterday, right?

Uncanny how things just up and disappear.

You whisper this in a hushed tone as if your wife is within hearing range. Anxiety like a court jester asks, "How's it going?"

Rolling around in a shoebox are six, high-base shotgun shells of the proper gauge for shooting tom turkeys. Their color and heft say big birds. Carry them to your camouflage vest that still hangs on the hook where you left it last year – surely a win – and drop the shells into the pockets like wheel bearings.

Inside the house you pull on a pair of flannel slippers and rummage in a storage bench for gear where you find the face net and your camo hats.

Another win.

You unpack the entire hunting tote onto the carpeted entryway floor and the dog, awake now, strolls over, stretches and shakes. He wants to ask if he's coming along but, sensing your uneven temperament, skulks to the dog bed to watch.

"Camo gloves anyone?" you say aloud, holding a half dozen pairs like the combs on a cartoon chicken. You return to the garage determined, now that you've warmed up and notched a few wins, to find the box calls and striker.

A gobble call – Eureka! – is located in a tote that says fishing gear.

The face paint is tucked into the toolbox with the box-end wrenches.

Lookit this! Voila! You say, and fish a bone-handled pocket knife you used to skin last year's tom from the pocket of a pair of jeans under three coats and two shirts on a hook.

A mourning dove coos quietly from the bird clock on the wall above the chest freezer. Before your wife many years ago relegated the clock to the garage, you could match the hour by the call of the many birds on its face.

Not any more.

All you know is that it's early. There's still time to make it to the woods.

You squint through the dim light and see how many minutes have passed since you began hurriedly gathering your gear for this morning hunt.

You cannot be dissuaded. You're on a roll now, racking up wins. How does it feel, you ask yourself, all this winning?

Two hours later, you're straddling a stool in the kitchen sipping coffee in a warm spot of sun and drawing squiggles on a paper pad.

You wish you were out there with your back to a tree, sitting in a holler listening for gobbles like your neighbor might be, but you're here instead, making a list.

"Find striker and box call," it says in stoically printed block letters. "Camo pants," it says. "Decoys and mouth calls."

Clean the garage, it says.

Clean your desk.

Your wife comes downstairs. She smiles brightly as you sip and haltingly scribble, averting your eyes.

"Thought you were hunting," she says merrily.

You nod furtively.

Feeling morose, you turn to look out the window at streams of sunshine drying the dew in the yard.

Then, as she turns to pour coffee, you add to the list:

"Get organized!"

Virgil In His Dale

It is one of those feuds that keeps the county sheriff's office in business.

Deputies spend the bulk of their time throwing water on fires like this.

They travel to the hollers after reports of gunplay and boundary disputes.

They drive the highway out of town and follow it through sweeping turns as it climbs wooded hillsides, passes clearcuts, follows a stream edge and drops to river bottoms, or skirts the shoreline of the small lakes that pock valleys like beer bottle tops.

The deputies veer their cars from arteries where the centerline is faint as an old tattoo onto bumpy gravel byways that are seldom graded and pocked with chuckholes.

They insulate the wheel wells of their patrol vehicles with fine clay dust, kicking up rocks, spilling lonely thoughts into clearings and shadowy canyons as the odometer clicks away.

The county officers key their mikes in places they know radio towers can hear them.

"Twenty-ten, I'm code four at twelve-mile Sheep Dip Creek."

There are two creeks with the same name on different sides of the county where Targhee raisers once waited out the seasons with their pot metal stoves and wall tents while summering their stock at higher ground. On either side of the divide that separates the national forest from the rolling prairies of the Palouse the slopes are green and timbered unlike the brackish plains of southern state. The land lies near the end of a sinewy goat trail of a state ighway. Its pavement cracks and washouts fill back pages of legislative agendas, but maintenance is seldom addressed.

The hippies who moved into the country in the age of Aquarius settled into the foothills and hollers after purchasing acres by mail order from the back of The Whole Earth Catalog. They threw up tepees and shacks that didn't last as long as the rough-lumbered corrals and ramps of the sheepherders.

Later, the marijuana growers cultivated their Benewah stash that was lauded in the pages of High Times, bringing the kind of notoriety that still finds sheriff's deputies sniffing creek bottoms in their attempts to locate dope.

The pot growers over the past few decades turned crack dealers and converted this mostly rural backwater into their meth-cooking mecca. From ridges and mountain overlooks they kneel every evening toward sunset with binoculars, scanning the gravel county roads – the only routes the axles of the deputy's patrol cars can handle.

Up here in Purgatory Gulch, where Virgil lives, that same history repeated itself.

Virgil's place is not too many miles from town, but the people, a lot of them back when Virgil moved in, had the shifty walk that meant they couldn't cross your property without stealing anything that wasn't tied down with a boom chain or welded to the bumper of your hay bine.

Virgil filed reports with law enforcement every few years when his feud with the neighbors tilted south.

His neighbors, it is documented, attempted at different times to run him off the five acres where he raises cur hounds for chasing cats and bears, a garden of onions and beans and tomatoes, a brown pony for his grandkids, and hell, a lot of the time.

"I ain't afraid of no man, and that's what gets me in trouble," Virgil says.

He is the kind of ageless hilljack you trust as honest and wouldn't want to cross despite his seventy-plus years. He's been that old for as long as I can remember and has been running two feuds for a quarter century, each with neighbors bordering different sides of his property.

"I told him, I said mister, if you don't walk away right now I'm liable to take that ten gauge out of my pickup and blow a hole in you so big they will have to bury you twice."

On a spring evening a while back, Virgil stirred a smoldering slash fire with a four-pronged pitchfork when a man who hired the county's most crooked attorney to steal Virgil's land came onto his property to threaten.

"He was edging pretty close, just getting meaner and meaner, and I looked at that pitchfork and at his belly and then I looked him in the eyes, and there was a moment of silence, if you know what I mean, and then he just turned tail and left dust running down my road."

Virgil has lost hounds to his neighbors. They shoot them from the tree line on the other side of his barbed-wire fence.

His complaints are hand-written entries in the sheriff's office blotter that recount property disputes, purloined timber, hay stolen or set ablaze. Most recently, his pony was shot with several rounds from a .22-caliber rifle, so he gave the animal away to be tended in a gentler place.

To replace his dogs he drives to relatives and friends in the Arkansas hill country where he lived before coming to Idaho for a job with the federal forest service back in the day.

He retired from it, supplemented his pension as a handyman and carpenter, and snuffed the fires that neighbors sparked around the slanted acreage on the gulch where he settled with his wife who has since died.

I say, "Virgil, these are the kinds of feuds I don't like."

I recall how a man – one of Virgil's neighbors – aggravated at my stance on an unrelated matter, threatened me with a Bowie knife.

Virgil looks at me from under a trucker cap, his face unshaven, his broken nose and the ears that flag and hang like satellite dishes. His glasses are askew, the lenses dusted. The dogs on the chains behind him watch with a gentleness that belies their ferocity in the face of angry bears or the cougars they chase in the mountains from here to the Silver Valley.

He spits.

"I don't like them neither, but what's a man to do," Virgil says, wiping his lips. "I'm no drinker, smoker or drugger, and that's what gets me in trouble."

Virgil's little piece of heaven gets as much snow as anywhere on the gulch. It occupies a nook between two high hills. Neighbors who moved in later, Virgil says, made a living selling dope. The peacocks they keep as watchdogs eat Virgil's garden beginning in spring as soon as the tender shoots push through the dirt, and the raiding continues into harvest time.

He could lay the birds down with a few shotgun bursts, but to keep the peace Virgil invariably calls sheriff's deputies instead.

He tells of an incident in which nearby residents, sheltered with anonimity, turned evidence on a neighbor and Virgil was subpoenaed. The subsequent raid turned up a few hundred marijuana plants on a parcel of sun-blotched land just up the road from Virgil's place. The perpetrators spent scant time in jail, then fingered Virgil for their misfortune.

"I keep to myself, mostly, if you know what I mean. There's a lot of good people moving in. They don't need this kind of garbage."

Neither does Virgil.

"Let's take a walk," he says.

It's early.

I met him in the grocery store in town this morning as I purchased pancake mix and coffee.

I followed his pickup up the winding dirt road through the tall pine and fir, into the gulch to his homestead.

Our breath curled in the still-frosty shade between the cedars alongside his driveway.

We walked to his hay pile where he pointed at two, large, burned holes.

"Roman candles, I think that's what it is."

Had the fireworks ignited the bales, the burn would have torched his house, a narrow utilitarian structure so immaculately clean, plumbed and square you could cut your finger on a corner.

"I don't know, pardner," he says. "I ain'ta leavin'."

He thinks he might escalate the feud because, after all, enough is enough.

"I've known the sheriff since he moved into the county hisself."

He understands the sheriff's hands are tied pending substantial evidence.

"What's an honest man to do, if you know what I mean?" Virgil asks.

He'll stick it out until his skin turns white and his eyes fall back into his head and they take him from the mountain he has called home most of his life.

"I've always been an honest man," he says.

Thanks for coming out to take a look at this malfeasance, Virgil says, holding out a hard, wide hand. I just wanted you to know the length and width of it.

"I got no one else to complain to, I guess," he says. "What's a man to do?"

I leave Virgil standing in a patch of morning sun, slightly bent, dust on his eyeglass lenses, his trucker's cap slightly askew, as cur hounds stand around him flop eared and docile waiting to be fed.

Fine clay dust coats my wheel wells as I go.

TANK CREEK

Fit To Float

His T-shirt says Shipwrecked Pete.

It stretches over a belly like plastic wrap over a melon.

He's glad to see me and smiles.

The once-handsome grin has gone toothless now.

He wants to know about my love life.

I'm sixty seven, he says.

"Let me be your father for a moment."

He doesn't tell me that his boat sank, but that's the reason
I'm here.

For more than a decade he worked to refurbish the thirty

six-foot wooden longliner that he purchased on the coast
and dragged back to Idaho to sit dry on barrels alongside
this downtown building in Harrison. He mended the vessel,
repaired its engine, caulked, replaced and waterproofed its
shiplap, decked its wheelhouse, foc'sle and small galley. He
added sonar, a cookstove and a marine radio.

And he covered much of it with paint.

Lots of paint.

On fine days in the off season when the town was not
graced with tourists, the high pitch of the sander or circular
saw rang down the street until someone yelled, "Pete, you
have a customer!"

The old sailor, who grew up in Germany and who went
to sea with the merchant marines as a young man, climbed
down a ladder propped against the gunwales, dusted himself
off and strolled smiling into the Steamboat Trader, his
sundry sporting goods shop in one of the town's historic
brick buildings.

Today, he smokes a filterless cigarette on the sidewalk
in front of The Trader and Bev's shop of yarn, knick knacks
and memorabilia.

Smoke curls blue into the day.

He smiles at me.

"You can trust a boat," he says. "You can't trust women. You
should know that by now."

He is not through giving advice.

"For every action there's an equal and opposite reaction,"
he says.

"You know who said that?" He grins at me.

A physicist, I say.

"Yes," he expounds. "Very good. A physicist who was old, like me."

He inhales and blows out a stream of cigarette smoke that dissipates into warm sunlight.

His boat, the one he bought for a thousand dollars on the coast and named Puffin, the one he said had beautiful lines, sank last night after its maiden run up the Coeur d'Alene River.

She was tied to the dock in the marina, a stone's throw from the back of Pete's shop, with the bilge pumps running while the swelling wood allowed water to seep into the hull before the boards snugged.

But the batteries ran low and the incoming rush of the lake burned up the bilge pumps, Pete says.

The wood swelled too slowly. Water filled the hull and overcame the mechanical effort of the pumps. They coughed, sputtered and gave in to nature's tenacious and unyielding superiority.

When Pete left the boat tied up in the evening the bilge pumps were shooting water nicely into the bay. The wooden seams were closing and the boat drafted the same as she had hours earlier, he says. But that night under a moon like lipstick and amidst a foggy veil like a spring wedding, the Pacific Puffin slowly and silently slipped into the frog water.

Only the wheelhouse protruded from the slack pool of Coeur d'Alene Lake like a periscope.

Pete stood on the dock the next morning with his hands in his pockets and a cigarette plugged into his mouth looking down at the sunken boat. The incident did not arouse premonition.

"Boats do what boats do," he said. And wooden boats sink before they float.

A small contingent of well wishers got her off the bottom, drained the water from the engine and replaced the pumps.

She's in fine shape now, he says. Even the Volvo motor that he calls a stump puller is cranking as if she's in the throes of courtship.

But women, he shakes his head, holding the filterless cigarette between two fingers.

"I still worry about my exes, and it's been thirty years."

The boat is his new love, the only woman who holds his attention, he says.

He smiles that smile. It is bashful and at the same time streetwise as a short-tailed cat.

"She's my baby," he says with a German accent that bears the sharpness of the Old Country despite the almost fifty years Pete has spent in the states.

A former sailor on vessels around the globe and an army interpreter for American troops in Vietnam, Pete worked the oil refineries after his discharge, punching clocks in shipyards before he bought into the tackle shop in Harrison years ago.

If there's one thing he knows, it's water and boats.

Women are like the sea, he says. If you have patience you can ride them out, but there's always another storm on the horizon.

He earned a piece of shrapnel and U.S. citizenship for his service in the green machine, he says, and lost a wife while he was in Southeast Asia.

He's sticking to boats and a little bit of wine that he drinks from a tall glass as he tends his main street shop in the brick building above the harbor at the mouth of the Coeur d'Alene River.

The wooden slats of the old longliner are sealed now tight as can be, so the bilge pumps only push a couple of gallons a day, he says.

This cheers him.

He is waiting on permits, so the vessel can be used as a work boat pulling beach logs. Those are the logs that have slipped from the brails of tug boats as they head to the mills on the Spokane River.

Once the sawlogs leave the brails, and become beached and unclaimed, they are free for the taking, he says.

Sun falls through the big windows of his shop warming the wooden floors. It dusts the gift aisle, the fishing lures, the fossils and gemstones he sells in small boxes, the life jackets, inflatable watercraft, paddles, oar locks and rope.

A woman enters through the door that is propped open. She needs a swim suit for her son.

"He's swimming at the beach in his jeans, right now," she says. "I don't want him to drown."

Futilely Pete shuffles through boxes of garments that appear to have been shipped in the 1970s from Sears and Roebuck.

"We don't have a wide selection," he replies.

He gives up his search and returns to the counter with a smile.

"You can have my underwear," he says. "They're boxers."

Boxers with boats on them.

"It looks like I'll have to drive to town," the woman replies, meaning she will travel to Coeur d'Alene for swimwear.

When she leaves through the shop's front door an electric buzzer sounds and Pete, standing by the cash register, raises the tall glass with the wine.

He addresses me by name, rolling the "R" as in his native tongue.

"Tell me about your love life," he says.

Ground Pounding For Trout

We were born worm fishermen and maybe as a way to untangle ourselves, that's how the other shoe will drop, with us slinging a worm on a hook through the surface of a blue-ribbon river famed as dry fly nirvana.

Such a turbulent undertaking may be abetted by a middle finger pressed into the air as the hot wind of retribution howls loud as a gully washer.

A pal of mine who mostly pursues simpler pleasures calls himself a part-time fly fisherman.

"The IPA drinking part," he says.

As a kid in the cow pasture, especially after a period of showers, he slipped around in pointy boots flipping patties looking for the androgenous boodle that squirmed underneath, dropping fistfuls of worms into a can.

He still on occasion pursues this uncomplicated amusement with an accent that slides effortlessly into his native cadence, all hick and sidearm.

"Man," he says, "I don't need to mess with that fancy stuff. I can just as easily drown a crawler on a number eight hook."

There's an attitude among worm danglers that says you can have your expensive rubber pants, nifty twelve-pocket vests bulging with fly boxes and intricately tied fur and feathers. We don't envy your triple polarized Catalina fashion statements for the eyes, or handmade, hardwood guide nets with rubber baskets to slog long-neck bottles of microbrew. Because, Bub, beer in cans is easier to pack and I can pull bigger fish with my bait and jorts than you can with your peacock herl and matching bandanna that keeps the sweat from running down your spine.

Laugh if you want, but don't let your voice crack.

At a country-club gathering not long ago, idle talk took an unexpected bounce and landed on the topic of fishing. Even among the effete, modesty was kicked to the curb and lines were drawn.

Tight lines, be assured, either way.

It was spin casters versus long rods, and any cogent argument was heavy with pecksniffian snickery.

The politics of fish nation found a hill of demagoguery to die upon.

I like dry flies, it's true. A lot of them. I like the long cast and the big whipping mend. I like the trout on the far side of a fast-moving river in spring that no one can reach. The ones you see, if you're patient, slurping the bugs that fall from the overhanging limbs of the tilting cedars.

They are often big, red-sided fish with a hooky mouth and

I'll wade to my chest in the current and float around the bend if I must, to land those hogs on a number five rod.

I wasn't always like this.

As a boy, days were doused with leeches and nightcrawlers, the whiff of arrowhead and pike grass was pungent as the day was soft. Weedless spoons going kerplunk caused a V-line of wake that meant a northern pike was on its way.

Bass, too, under a sultry moon with the AM radio crooning quietly and a plug gurgling until you heard the splash before you saw it. The smallmouths at the end of the line were all pull and vinegar.

Last week on Montana's St. Regis River I met a man with an accent so East Coast it could bake beans. He had returned from spending a day on the other side of the mountain sacking fish in Idaho water.

Over there, he expounded, he was catching trout with every cast.

"As many as I wanted to take," he zoused.

His fly rod was the one you admire in the catalogs, but won't shell out payments to own. His gear, vests, fly boxes, waders and boots, and one of those Australian hats made from the fur on the inside of a kangaroo's pouch were freshly minted and the medley was shipped to Montana via Air-Express. He had it delivered to his hotel room door.

"How did you lure those wild trout?" I inquired. "Dry flies?"

Negative, he retorted, peering over the metallic frames of tinted Cape Lagunas.

"This here dealie."

He drew a big cone-headed fur and feathered puffball from his pocket that begged for a rabies shot.

Michael Jackson sang "Ben" to appease this thing.

What is it? I asked, stupefied.

It has a funny name, the man said.

"They are ugly to cast but boy, do they fish."

The four-inch articulated rag of steel and facial hair was not really a fly, it was bait.

It was second cousin to a vibrating spinner with a chrome bumper and horn that went honk.

It was a lure, but it might as well have been a squiggling sculpin, or a vole fresh from a cow pasture and snelled to a sinker.

He handed me one.

"Take it," he said. "I got more."

I carried the gadget to the river on my dashboard expecting it to leap for the open window and dive out.

When I rolled to a stop alongside the Idaho stream the man had fished earlier, I threaded the eye of the lure, made a knot and walked to the bank adjusting my chichi, white-framed, gangsta, gas station shades. Standing splay legged on a gravel bar in cut-offs and flip flops, I sent the gizmo sailing over the water in bolo fashion.

In a nice run where a while back no trout rose to my small, tightly-wrapped hair flies I caught three of the fattest cutthroat trout a sunburned man with jerky breath could want.

As daylight faded, bull bats flashed in the still air.

I was a fly fisherman, sure.

But as my line zipped back and forth through the eyes on my moderately priced single-handed rod, and as cars on the road slowed down for the drivers to jeer at my cast, I paid them no mind.

With a couple of cans of warm brew stowed in my pockets, I was catching big ones.

Dragging bottom.

I was chucking bait.